I0778539

Castlebound Adventures

Rats in the Cellar!

Eric Kercher

Paper and Sword, LLC

FROM THE AUTHOR

There are days when we all need an escape from a terrible job, a terrible day, or a terrible life.

Join my newsletter and get an escape from the real world, stories, and lore designed to entertain and delight.

You'll also get *Stories from the Deep*, an exclusive, unpublished anthology chock full of extra epilogues, short stories, and lore from the Patmos Sea Fantasy Adventure Series.

Join now at erickercher.com.

Enjoy the book.

-Eric Kercher

1

WASHED UP ON THE ISLE

Neil clutched at the package, taking the steps two at a time. Sirens screamed somewhere in the distance, the sounds of the neighbors shouting at each other punctuated by loud bangs.

Finally, he was at his apartment. The door slid open at his touch, then jammed three quarters of the way like usual.

He let out a few expletives, then tried to force it open. It refused to move, so he had to try to squeeze through, huffing and puffing, trying to pull in his gut.

It caught as he was almost through, then he strained and groaned. Sweat poured down his face, then he popped through and fell, sprawling on the floor.

Neil groaned, then a shock of fear ran through him. His fingers searched the grimy floor, then closed around his package.

He stood, hands trembling, not wanting to see. "Lights," he said.

They faded on. The package was intact, and he turned it over to make sure. A wave of relief flooded through him.

He kicked the front door, and it unstuck enough to close and lock. His hunger forced him to grab a plastic bag of stuffed pockets and a few slices of leftover pizza. While he was there, he added a few bags of potato chips and an extra-large Soda Slam.

The bag was half empty by the time he made it through the small galley kitchen into his bedroom. He pushed aside a few dirty clothes on his bed and sat down, taking the console from its premium storage tank on the bedside table.

The chips crunched, flooding his mouth with salt and potato, and helped to calm him from the near miss.

The food went on the floor, and he wiped the grease on his pant legs, making sure his hands were clean.

Then, he took the package and held it up, a ritual that he took seriously. The plastic gleamed in the LED light, the curtains drawn to prevent any other source of impure light.

"Castlebound Adventures," he whispered. Above him something slammed and the arguing picked up again.

It was Friday, and he didn't have to be back to work for another three days. He sighed, smelling the game.

It had that crisp, new plastic smell that he loved. He ripped the side of the plastic, crinkling it up into a ball he tossed onto the floor.

This was supposed to have the top of the line graphics and the most immersive story line of any RPG on the market. He had spent days pouring over reviews on the net, watching demos and sneak peeks of combat and exploration.

They had included an olfactory special too, something the last patch had rolled out. That extra bit of hardware had set him back a bit, but he was hoping it was worth it.

Now, disrobed, the case was ready for the first opening. Neil held his breath and wrapped a sausage finger around the side and pressed down.

It clicked.

Inside was a simple square, a sword emblazoned on it in silver. He gasped, holding it gently with trembling fingers and watching it shine.

It was beautiful.

He couldn't wait anymore, not even to eat, and he slipped it into the console, put the mask on his face, and laid down.

The mask blocked out all aspects of the outside world, connecting in to his brain stem. The sounds of his apartment and the yelling faded away, the light from the LEDs fading to black. Even the smells went away, something he had never felt before.

And then, that simple chime, and the soothing voice of a woman. "Welcome."

A world rushed by, a blur of greens, browns, and blue. For a second he thought he saw a mountain, steaming with smoke, but then it was gone.

He was...on an island. There was no other way to put it.

Waves crashed against the beach a few feet in front of him. He looked down, wriggling his fat toes in the sand. It was coarse, and rough, and stuck between his toes.

And he could feel all of it.

But that wasn't it either. He could smell the sea salt in the air, and a tropical flower hint just below it.

Wind ruffled his hair.

"Traveler." A voice behind him made him whirl. Back in his apartment he wasn't moving a hair, but it felt like every muscle in his body was reacting to his commands.

No lag this time, glad that patch cleared it up. A man was standing behind him on the beach, clad in full armor except a helm, a great dragon emblazoned on his chest in gold.

"My name is Sir Drandel Mavaret." He leaned his head forward in a small bow. "And I am to ease your way back into the world."

"The world?"

Mavaret swept his hand across the land behind him, armor clinking softly in a happy melody. His demeanor was calm, a striking difference to his scarred face and hair graying at the temples. "The world of Enthera. We found you on the beach, washed up with little on you but rags. We assumed you had been washed ashore from a shipwreck, but you've been asleep until today."

Neil was expecting a menu, or a prompt of some sort, but there was nothing but the luscious, tropical landscape and this strange man in front of him.

"Er..." Neil scratched his head. "Am I supposed to create my avatar first, or something?"

"Avatar?" Mavaret looked puzzled. "I'm unfamiliar with your language."

"Never mind," he mumbled.

"What is your name, traveler?"

Ah, this is how you start, I see. "Call me..." He had to think of something good, no use using his real name. *What would I be called if I were a real knight?* "Call me Lancelot."

"Very well, Lancelot." Mavaret reached out his hand. Neil cringed a bit, but he had always liked stories of knights and King Arthur, and Neil didn't have the same kind of ring to it. "Well met."

Neil took Mavaret's hand, which he promptly regretted as the man's grip was harder than iron. "Yes, well met." He shook his hand, trying to get the blood flowing back into it.

"Come this way, we have equipment ready for you." Mavaret turned and headed to a stone path that went into the jungle, and Neil perked up. *Equipment sounds promising.*

The man was quiet on the trip, which Neil hated. "How long have you been here? Say, where is here anyway?"

"This island is called Clearwater." Mavaret ducked under a low-hanging branch. "I've lived here for the last three years."

The armor didn't seem to bother him, and Neil wondered at that. He was already feeling tired, which was strange for a game. They must have had some sort of fatigue mechanic built in. Either way, it didn't help him to stop breathing heavily other than to stop every so often on the gentle climb up the hill.

"Clearwater. Sounds nice," he said after another short break. Mavaret was waiting for him, looking back every so often. It didn't seem to bother him to stop.

"Yes, it is a beautiful island, nothing like my homeland." The man stared off into the distance. "As I'm sure you feel just as keenly. You'll get your strength back soon."

"Good." They kept going. Neil marveled at the graphics, everything looked so lifelike and real. He reached out and touched the leaf of a plant.

It was waxy, and smooth. His fingers came back with a small amount of residue on it, and chills went down his back.

The level of detail in this game is amazing.

"Here we are." Neil heard a small ringing as they entered a clearing. A group of small buildings ringed around a small square, each made of tropical wood and covered in a palm leaf roof.

Most had their sides open and exposed. Neil caught a glimpse of a smithy, from which issued the clanging, and a kitchen, as well as a strange set of glasses.

"Welcome to the town of Redemption," Mavaret said. "Come, we have a place for you over here."

Men and women were hard at work, but they glanced up and stared at him. Neil looked down. He had only a small pair of shorts and a rough shirt on.

And, to his disappointment, he still had his build. Neil reddened, and shrank down to be as inconspicuous as possible.

Mavaret led him to a small building filled with doors. Behind the closest one was a small cot, a table, and a chair, all made out of teak.

"You may use this to store anything you produce or collect, for the time being, but we must warn you this will not be available for long. You need to leave this place within a month."

A month? Shouldn't be too bad. "Ah."

"We've also provided you with some basic supplies. I'll let you get changed." Mavaret shut the door behind him.

On the bed was a set of clothes. Neil approached it, unsure of how to handle it. Usually games had some sort of instructions, but this one wasn't like any other game he had played.

He crouched down, looking for instructions closer in, but there was nothing. He waved a hand over them.

Nothing.

The island felt warm, with a light breeze blowing in through an open window carrying the smell of flowers with it. It all felt so real, so what if the equipment was the same?

He went to pick it up. His fingers touched the fabric. It was rougher than his own t-shirts, but not the worst thing he had ever felt.

It acted like a normal shirt when he picked it up, fell apart from the folds and hung between his fingers.

Neil took off his old shirt and put on the new one. It fit better around the shoulders, but the waist was a bit more snug.

"Just like a normal shirt." The pants were the same way, brown breeches made of a strange cloth he had never seen before. It came with a belt which he wrapped around his waist and cinched up.

As he dressed, he looked around. This was the strangest game he had ever played. No instructions, no manual. How was he supposed to get to the menus?

There had to be some way.

The last thing on the bed were some soft moccasin-looking shoes. When he picked them up he noticed something strange beneath them.

It was a small amulet, made of a cheap tin or something similar, coiled up underneath the shoes.

"Hello, what do we have here?" Neil picked it up, but the moment he touched it something strange ran through his body, like a jolt of electricity.

Words materialized on the oval tin amulet. *Lancelot*.

"This must be it," he murmured. Neil slipped it around his neck. It was cool on his skin, the chain made of the same flimsy material.

He finished dressing and looked around at the empty room. Behind the door was a small shelf, nothing on it. Other than that, the room was sparse.

Neil sat down on the bed and lifted the amulet up. A small chime sounded and light shone from it. It grew until it was floating up above him, turning into a circular interface.

That made him feel better because down at the bottom of it was a small logout button. He was beginning to feel a sense of dread. The place was too real.

Other than the logout button, there was a small one in the middle in a plain font. He tried touching the light, but nothing happened until he tried to swipe it to the side.

There were a list of skills, little icons differentiating them. Sword, staff, and a small hammer.

He gave a small laugh of relief. "So this is where it is." They were there all at once, except one strange icon with no text next to it. That was set at ten.

He wondered at that, but a knock at the door interrupted him. There wasn't an obvious way to dismiss the menu, even though he flipped through them furiously, but not fast enough for Sir Mavaret to open the door.

"Uh, how do I get rid of this?"

"I see you've discovered the amulet you came with. I'm afraid I don't know what you're talking about."

Neil pointed to the glowing light in front of him. "You can't see this?"

"See what?" Mavaret stood, eyes transfixed on him as if he were growing horns out of his skull.

"Never mind," Neil said sheepishly, a hint of blush coming to his cheeks.

"If you'll follow me, I can get you acquainted with our village."

Neil nodded and followed, trying to get the menu to go away. Finally, he tapped the amulet and words materialized.

Close menu?

"Yes." Nothing happened. Neil tried tapping the amulet again. The circle shrank, then turned into a ball of light that dove back into the amulet.

Neil breathed a sigh of relief, then tucked the amulet under his shirt. *Best not lose this then.*

"You'll be staying in the men's quarters with us. Over there are the women's quarters." Mavaret pointed to a similar shaped rectangular building filled with doors to his right.

"And over here is the dining hall. It isn't much, but we eat well for who we are." The hall was just off to the side of the men's quarters, three sides open with a fireplace made out of an orange stone on the other. Poles of what looked like a thin tree held up the roof. "Behind it is the kitchen. Most stay out, but you're welcome to try your hand at cooking. Mary is our head cook and can get you started."

A woman with brown hair turned and nodded to them, then returned to her work kneading bread.

"You'll find we're a simple village, we don't have much, but we survive. We gather most of our materials from areas just around the village and bring them here." Mavaret stopped at a squat building without windows. "This is the warehouse and holds everything we need, including our food. It's off limits for now, but prove yourself and you will gain access to some of the supplies inside."

Neil tried to look inside, but the door was shut with an iron lock on it and Mavaret didn't seem keen on opening it.

"Can we go inside?" Neil asked. Mavaret shook his head.

"We'll continue to the smithy." He turned and walked over to the building emitting the most amount of smoke.

A forge stood off to one side, an anvil in the center. The ringing came from the smith at his work, smashing a hunk of glowing metal as another younger man worked the bellows of the forge. He stepped on a platform, which sent sparks from the fire, and tongues of flame, then released it and it died down.

Neil went inside, curious as to what the smith was making.

"This is Smith the Blacksmith," Sir Mavaret said. "He can show you how to craft and forge."

The big man stopped hammering and jabbed the metal back into the fire. He turned back to Neil, looked down at him, and nodded.

"Nice to meet you," Neil said, extending a hand. Smith grunted, then returned to his work.

There was a table next to him, what looked like recently completed items on it. Neil edged closer, taking a look out of the corner of his eye while Mavaret pointed out parts of the smithy he could use.

There was a small knife, little more than a dagger, but it caught Neil's eye. It looked sharp, razor sharp almost, and gleamed in the light of the fire.

He reached out and touched it, but pain flared in his hand and he snatched it back. Neil's eyes opened wide in shock.

Pain?

2

MARK OF THE DRAGON

Neil stared at his hand. It throbbed, almost like it was real pain.

"Hot," Smith said, shaking his head. Neil couldn't tell if it was in disappointment or in laughter, the man's face was as iron as the metal he worked.

"Why isn't the pain going away?" Neil asked. A great, red welt bloomed in the shape of the knife blade. He was glad he hadn't touched the sharp side.

"Pain lingers until it is healed," Mavaret said. "Here." He reached into a satchel at his waist and wrapped something around Neil's reddened hand.

It went to work quickly, the pain sapping away. It felt cool and smooth, but the back of it was scratchy.

"Keep that on it while we continue on." Mavaret nodded towards the smiths and went back outside.

Neil followed him, taking off the strange compress. He sniffed it. It had a smell he had never smelled before, but vaguely reminded him of cooking.

"Down that path you'll find the mines, but you shouldn't go there on your own."

Neil looked up from the bandage and down a well-trodden path that led into the jungle. Behind it was a small rise and a rocky outcropping. He supposed that was where they were, but it had to be less than a mile away.

"Mines?" Neil asked, perking up. He had heard the crafting system was complicated, and lifelike, but fun.

"Yes. And here is the farm plot." Mavaret stopped outside a plot of dirt. A man was in the center, tilling the earth. It gave off a wonderful smell, and Neil wanted to reach down and run his hands through it, but restrained himself.

Small shoots of green poked up through the furrows, some even had small leaves on them. "We grow everything we eat and don't catch. Farmer Bill can help you learn," Mavaret said.

Bill stopped tilling and raised his reed hat, then bowed. "Welcome to come try your hand."

"I'd like that." Beyond the farm plot were a series of planted bushes growing in a line, then trees after that. Some of them had been cut down, stumps leaving a mark of their existence, and an axe was stuck in the top of one.

There was so much to learn, and so many places to explore. Neil breathed in the fresh air, smelling the tropical flowers and hint of sea salt and wood smoke.

Neil's eyes lingered on the axe. He wondered, after all of this introduction, when he would be able to use anything.

"I see you want to try your hand with it. Go on, take it." Mavaret waved him on.

"I can?" Neil asked. Mavaret nodded.

The axe, when he got closer, wasn't actually an axe. It was a smaller hatchet, but when he picked it up it was heavy in his hand. He swung it a few times.

"Like this," Mavaret showed him how to use it, and gave him a few pointers on how best to use his arms to continue the power.

A small chime sounded. "What was that?" Neil asked, looking around.

"I didn't hear anything." Mavaret was staring at him strangely. Farmer Bill had gone back to his work tilling. Neil realized what it was and dug back into his shirt to pull out the amulet.

He flipped over to the skills menu. Sure enough, the axe skill had gone up to a resounding two.

"It's my highest skill," Neil said, beaming. More than a bit proud, he swung the hatchet around a few more times.

"Why don't you try it on the tree? We could use a little more firewood," Mavaret said.

Neil stepped up to the small tree, barely more than a sapling, and gave it a swing. His hatchet gouged into the bark, then bit into the wood.

Neil pulled it back out and tried again, this time missing his first hit. He tried again, a little bit closer to the first one, but still off.

A few more swings finally got him feeling his swing better and a few more chops after that the tree cracked and leaned, then fell to the ground.

"Good. You can collect it here and we'll take it back to the wood storage later. Come on."

"Where are we going?" Neil looked down at the wood, wondering what it was for. Could it be used for crafting of some sort?

The ideas rushed through his head. It would make a good shaft for an axe, or maybe the start of a piece of furniture. He longed to try and make something out of it, but Mavaret was already on the move.

He slipped into the forest, down another well-trodden path. Neil followed, pushing vegetation and leaves out of his way. Bugs buzzed around his head, an annoyance Neil wasn't sure he enjoyed.

They went a few minutes down it before the forest thinned and then they were in a small clearing, a waterfall just across the distance from them.

Fog rose from the pool at the bottom, sending up a sprinkle of rainbows that reflected in the afternoon sun.

"This is where you can fish, if you have the equipment. It is an important source of food for the village," Mavaret said. He had stopped at the edge of the pool.

Neil looked down into it, the bottom visible in the crystal-clear water. Fish of some sort he had never seen before swam and turned, a dark red that almost blended in with the sand on the bottom.

"Fishing? I never really liked doing that." Neil recalled a game he had dedicated to it. It was insufferably boring.

"You may learn to like it, in time. There are many special types of fish in Enthera, some more useful than others." Mavaret raised one eyebrow, and Neil cocked his head to the side.

"Useful?"

"You can also gather materials in this area. The soil is particularly good for crafting, as it is a hearty clay that holds its shape well."

"Good to know," Neil said. He was staring up at the waterfall, taking it all in. It was beautiful, far more lifelike than anything else he had seen in other games.

"And it brings peace to those who rest here." Mavaret stooped down, then put his hand under a strange-looking plant near the shore. "This is hollyhock, an herb with healing properties. Gather some and bring it back with us, I have something to teach you."

"Gather it?" Neil knelt down to join him. "How do I do that?"

"Pick it, pinching it here above a split on the stem." Mavaret pointed to a notch where one stem branched out from another. He gave a quick pinch, and the smell from it filled the air with its fragrance.

"It smells good," Neil said, breathing it in. It had a faint smell of a soap he had used once, long ago when he was a boy. The thought of his childhood broke some of the spell of the game, reminding him of things he would rather forget. He frowned.

"Come, we'll go back to the village and I'll show you how to make healing supplies. You'll need them," Mavaret said, a strange tone to his voice. "Pick a few more."

Neil complied, cutting a few more branches off of the small plant, and soon heard another chime.

When he swiped to his skills, he found there was one glowing.

Herbalism.

A strange skill, and one he hadn't read about in the release material. *What good will that do me?*

But he finished picking a few more and followed Mavaret back to the village. The smell of them lingered on his hands, not unpleasant.

He enjoyed feeling the newness of this world, of being able to escape the life he'd rather not think about, but that thought made him go back to it.

It was already Friday, the first day of his weekend, and he had spent most of it going into Shinjuku just to pick the game up, and wait in line like everyone else, but he had been one of the few lucky ones with a reserved copy.

The others, not as much.

Anyone who hadn't reserved a copy had been out of luck, and not too pleasant to deal with.

Like his own boss on Monday.

Neil shivered, then tried to forget it. The sun on his back helped, and the arrival back in the village did too.

It was filled with life, and no one seemed worried or out to get anyone else. This was a place he could get used to, a place he could call home.

Strange, a home. Even more spartan than my own room.

There was more to come, though. There had to be, judging from the early release footage. He hadn't even gotten to the fighting tutorial yet.

And that, that was where the game was supposed to shine.

Mavaret showed him through the rest of the village, a few more spots for crafting and study, and even a small shop area where he could buy and sell things for small coins of bronze.

"What can I do with these?" Neil held up the herbs, bunched up in his hand.

"You'll need to carry much on your journeys, and I'm afraid you've lost your pack, if you ever had one." Mavaret motioned to the warehouse. "We have the supplies to make your own. Perhaps this is the first task I can assign you. Do you accept?"

Neil's amulet warmed. He touched it, and parchment materialize in front of him.

Craft a pack. Accept by mark.

Beneath that was a line, empty.

Am I supposed to sign it? Neil looked around for a pen or something, but there was nothing in sight. His cheeks started to burn as Mavaret stared at him.

This was the first hiccup so far, but it was embarrassing that Neil was stuck on the first quest. *How am I supposed to do this?*

"Yes. I accept." Neil felt like he wanted to crawl into a hole. Nothing happened, and the air went out of him. "Quest accepted."

Make your mark, the words glowed.

"How am I supposed to do that?"

"A mark is your symbol," Mavaret said, as if it was supposed to be helpful.

"I don't know what my symbol is? Am I supposed to sign?"

"A mark is your symbol." Mavaret was still staring at him, and Neil felt like all the characters were looking at him too. He reached out, trying to sign it with his finger.

As soon as his finger touched the page, a bell tolled. A circle of red appeared at the bottom, right on the line, and out of it grew a complex system of growing curves and lines. They overlapped, intersected, but he couldn't see what they were making.

Until it was complete.

Neil stared at it. Was this his mark?

"Good." Mavaret took up the parchment and looked at the bottom.

His eyes narrowed. "This is your mark?" His voice was harsh, strangely so. Gone was the kindly adviser, and in his place a battle-hardened veteran who was eyeing him like an enemy.

Cold chills grasped at Neil's throat, and he took a step back, holding up his hands. "I don't know what it was, it just showed up."

"A dragon. Your mark is a dragon," Mavaret said through clenched teeth. He advanced one step. "Is this how you treat me? After everything we've done to keep you alive, bring you back to health?"

Neil was trembling now, uncontrollably. "I don't know what happened. You have to believe me. Please."

His pleading brought a change to Mavaret, who stopped going forward at least. "You claim you didn't choose this mark?"

"No. It just happened."

A few agonizing moments passed. The anger in Mavaret's eyes slowly faded, and his kindly demeanor returned. "I believe you." He gave Neil one last glance before he rolled up the parchment and tucked it somewhere in his armor.

Neil breathed a sigh of relief and tried to calm himself. He snorted. Here he was, in a game, and he was worried about his safety.

But he couldn't shake that feeling when he saw the murder in Mavaret's eye. What had he done?

He had to hurry to catch up to Mavaret, who was already at the warehouse and inside. He emerged a second later with a bundle of cloth and thread.

"Take these." Mavaret offered them. "Take them to the crafting shop, Tanner will show you how to make your pack."

Neil took them, struggling to keep everything together, and went in the direction Mavaret had indicated.

The short interaction had left him unsettled, and when he glanced back he half expected the old knight to be stalking him like a jungle cat.

What he didn't expect was for Mavaret to be walking in the completely opposite direction.

"Wait, where are you going?"

"Meet me in the dining hall when you're finished." Mavaret didn't even turn around to say it.

Neil felt a little spike of fear, but then quickly smothered it. *It's only a game.*

Not to mention he saw Tanner there, just up ahead. He was drawing something across a hide stretched tight in a frame, strings holding it at all the sides.

"Tanner?"

"'Aht's me." The man swiveled around, peering at him with large, owlish eyes. "'A'd ya 'ant?"

Neil was taken aback at the rapid blinking. "Er, I have this."

"So?"

"I've come to learn how to make my pack."

"Ah, 'hy didn't you say so?" The man stood from his stool and took the supplies out of Neil's hands, spreading them along the workbench beside him.

He walked Neil through the tools, although to be honest Neil already knew what a needle and thread was.

Tanner, however, wasn't happy about Mavaret's selection and told him so. "Threads is completely useless in leather this thick. 'Hat 'e need is a good, thick thong, like this." He rummaged around under his bench until he grasped a roll of thin strips of leather, holding triumphantly in the air. "Behold, this 'ill 'ork better."

Neil tried to suppress a smile. Something about the man was amusing, but endearing at the same time.

They spent the next few hours in work as Tanner walked him through the basics. Although dry at times, Tanner's mannerisms and strange speech made it more interesting, and Neil barely even noticed his hunger until they were finished with the pack.

"Done," Neil said, pulling the leather thong through the last hole in the pack and tying it off. Another chime sounded, and he rushed to see what level he had gained.

It was in leather working, right next to metalworking and clothworking.

"That's it?"

Tanner nodded. "Finished."

Neil thanked him, and put it on. It fit well, and he forgot it as soon as he put it on, like it was always there.

Having completed his task, Neil started to go to the dining hall when his hunger reminded him it was there with a gurgle in his stomach.

How long have I been playing? There wasn't an in game clock for him to tell the time, but it had to be a few hours already, if not more.

He thought about going on, but then decided against it. *I can come back to it tomorrow.*

Neil pulled out his amulet and pulled his way to the logout screen. It asked him to confirm, which he hesitated on, but then pressed down on yes.

The world faded to black, then he was in his bed.

It was dark in his room, and dark outside, and that groggy sensation he had from a long amount of time in virtual reality hit him like a plank.

Neil pulled off the set, blinking in the blackness to try to get his vision back.

He turned over, looking at the clock on his bedside table. 2:36 a.m.

In the morning? How long have I been playing?

It had to have been at least six hours, even longer. The sun wasn't going down until 8 o'clock, and he was in before sundown.

And he was tired. It rolled over him at once, like it had been held off by the game. It fought his hunger, but his hunger won out and he shambled to the kitchen to grab a few more pieces of cold pizza.

They weren't great, and the crust was stale, but it was better than nothing. Neil ate it alone, then pushed all the junk off his bed and crawled under the covers.

He was still thinking about Castlebound Adventures, and how real it had felt. Almost more real than his apartment.

He would have a lot to do tomorrow in game, and a part of him tingled in anticipation, but he pushed it aside.

His body was too tired after his week of work, and he needed rest. Neil turned over and slipped off into sleep, dreaming of what was to come.

3

BACK TO **R**EALITY

Neil stepped off the train and into the station, his feet weighing him down. He looked up at his building, a breath catching in his throat.

Another day. I can make it through today. He took a deep breath, then walked into the rush of commuters.

The city was a cacophony of sounds. Horns blaring, people talking and shouting, alarms ringing. He bumped and pushed along with the crowd, trying to be as unimposing as possible, which was hard with his weight.

He didn't break down with anxiety, even though it was growing, and made it up through the elevator to his desk without being noticed.

Neil heaved a sigh of relief and slumped into his chair, which gave an ominous creak. Phones were ringing already, and he unloaded his snacks into his desk and pulled out his headset.

His first call was terrible. The old lady on the other end kept calling him rude names even though he was trying to help her. He sat there and took it. He had to, or the consequences would be harsh.

Dave had been fired the other week just for trying to defend himself. He wasn't the first, and he wouldn't be the last.

"I understand, we'll try to sort the problem out," Neil said.

"Try, you sniveling piece of trash," she screeched into his ear. "You've been trying for ten minutes and haven't even heard a word I've said."

She continued, adding a few choice words that were impolite in female company, and Neil clenched his teeth and ignored it.

Or tried to.

Each little insult was a spike that dug under his flesh.

By the time he had helped her a half hour was past, and his metrics were flashing red. His heart sank when Goltan's door opened. For a brief second he thought it would be someone else.

But then that goofy flop of hair turned his way and came down the aisle.

Neil scrolled through the list, trying to find a call to connect with. He clicked on a random name.

Blocked.

His heart sank. All he could do was wait.

"Neil, get in my office."

"Yes, Mr. Goltan." Neil stood, wishing he was back in the world of Enthera, or Gilet, or even a retro world.

Instead, he followed the pugnacious little man into his office as he slammed the door behind him.

All eyes briefly turned toward him, through the glass window that Goltan left open for all to see.

"First call of the day and you had to screw it up?" Goltan was chewing on gum. It didn't help his breath. "How many times do I have to tell you we're winners? Failing calls are what losers do, isn't it?"

"Yes, Mr. Goltan."

"Say it."

"Failing calls is for losers."

"That's right." Grady Goltan was in his face now, looking up at him with reddening cheeks. He poked a finger in his chest. It didn't feel good. "You want to end up on the street, you keep it up. I could have a million more of you in a heartbeat, but I keep you around out of the kindness of my heart."

Neil kept his eyes firmly fixed on the window outside. The sky was blue, he noticed, with barely a cloud in the sky. Everyone was watching him, he could feel their eyes on his back.

And the volume of Goltan's voice was increasing. "So you're going to listen up, and you're going to listen good. We help people, we lead them, and if you can't get your act together then you are a waste of space."

More finger jabbing. More pain in Neil's chest. He wanted to reach out and stop him, but he just stood there instead.

He screamed more. Neil tried to tune it out, thinking about what the quest rewards were going to be. He wondered about what was outside the island, what kind of world Enthera would be.

And he wondered why his mark was a dragon.

"Now get out of my office!" a red-faced Goltan bellowed, yanking open the door. As Neil almost ran to his cubicle, Goltan yelled to the rest of the watching room. "And the same goes for the rest of you. Under perform at your own risk!"

Neil's cheeks burned, and he kept his head down. Somehow he made it to his cubicle without melting in shame.

Somehow.

The rest of the morning was better. Not great, but better. Goltan kept scowling at him as his metrics steadily improved, until they were almost orange by lunch.

When the clock struck noon Neil was already up and headed for the door. A quick trip down the elevator to the cafeteria later and he was sitting down with a plate of food.

Bob saw him and joined, greeting him.

Neil tried to be cordial back, but he must have been a little curt.

"What's wrong?" Bob asked. "Is it because you got called into the principal's office?"

"You heard about that already?" Neil's face fell.

Bob shrugged. "You know how fast word travels around here."

"First call of the day." Neil shook his head slowly and took another bite of his hamburger. It was fine, but he chewed methodically. "I can't wait to get out of here."

"I didn't see you on the net all weekend."

"I got it."

Bob stopped eating, a forkful of macaroni and cheese halfway to his mouth. "No, you couldn't have."

Neil beamed. "Had to go to Shinjuku to get it, but they had an advanced sale."

"I can't believe it." Bob tilted his head. "You are serious. How is it?" He leaned in.

"Amazing. The smells really pull you into the game. I almost forgot I was in one the graphics were so good."

"You're lucky, I didn't even have access to that upgrade, let alone the moolah to make it happen."

"Gotta make sure you change your priorities. I don't have a fish tank to dump money into," Neil grinned.

"Leave Bessie out of this," Bob warned. Neil didn't try to push it, he seemed genuinely taken aback at the comment.

"Is everything okay?"

"No, she's sick and I can't figure out why." Bob took a sip from his drink. "She won't swim like she used to. She's sluggish and slow, like she's weighed down by something."

"Sounds bad."

"I've tried everything. I'm going to have to take her to the vet soon."

Neil wondered what it was like to have something dependent on you. His family had a cat once, but that was when he was really young and couldn't remember it well.

But to have something that relied on you for survival, for food and drink? He wondered at it.

"I hope she gets better soon." Neil stuffed his hamburger in his mouth.

"Thanks, I don't want to talk about it anymore."

Fine by me.

"Tell me about Castlebound Adventures," Bob said, still sporting a slightly sad look.

Neil smiled and launched into it, "I haven't even gotten past the first tutorial, but it feels real, I can tell you that. They even have pain receptors that make injuries hurt."

Bob's brows bunched up. "Really? I haven't heard about that before."

"It must be a new mod they're keeping hush hush, on the QT."

"Hmm..."

"Anyway--" The rest of the lunch hour flew by, with his excitement and Bob's questions. the bell rang, signaling the end of it, and Neil groaned.

"You'll have to tell me more," Bob said, dumping his trash into the trashcan.

"Will do," Neil said, following him. He caught a glimpse of someone walking by, and his heart skipped a beat.

He pulled up short. There she was.

"Neil, you coming?" Bob asked, turning. "Oh man."

"What's she doing down here?" he whispered. Great flowing locks of hair, those flashing blue eyes, it made him almost melt down to the vinyl tiles beneath his feet.

"You still can't be crushing on her."

The way she glided, like she was walking on water, made his heart palpitate furiously. Then, he realized she was coming this way, down the hall to their location.

"I..I..." there was nowhere to go. She would see him, all 250 pounds.

Her heels clicked on the tile, a staccato tune that drove straight into his brain. His feet were frozen to the floor.

Then, for half a second, she glanced his way and their eyes met. Disgust passed across hers, and she looked away in a heartbeat.

Then, she was past them, the lilac scent of her perfume lingering. Neil wanted to slink into the trashcan and close the lid.

"Why do you do this to yourself? Veronica is a raging--"

"Don't say it, not in my presence."

"Well she is," Bob said. "And what is she even doing down here? She's supposed to be on the seventh floor with all the rest of them." He waved his hand like he was wafting off a bad scent.

"Maybe..." Neil hazarded a glance down the hall, but she was gone. He left the rest unspoken, but hoped it with all his heart.

"She wouldn't give you the time of day even if you were the last man alive in the world." Bob took him by the shoulders, reaching up and shaking him lightly. "Snap out of it man. Rejoin reality."

Neil mumbled something he hoped would mollify Bob. It didn't.

"I've gotta go. I'll talk to you later." Bob gave him one last piercing glance, then left.

Neil didn't want to go back to his cubicle, but a quick glance at his watch and the deserted cafeteria made him realize what a storm of trouble he would be in if he didn't make it back and he hurried off to the elevators.

Bob was already getting into one, going down.

"Remember what I said." The door closed on him.

The elevators were all at different floors and Neil pushed the up button, clicking it a few times even though it was giving a weak, yellow glow.

He only had five minutes left. The indicators above the elevators were all at different floors, none of them close by.

This is going to be close. His palms started to sweat, and he wiped them on his pants to dry off.

A minute ticked by. Bob's elevator was coming back.

"Come on, come on," he urged. It dinged softly and Neil rushed in.

It smelled like the fake leather on the walls, and he jabbed the button a few times, pressing the door close button.

He was down to three minutes.

The doors creaked closed and the elevators started moving.

Thirty seconds later the chime dinged and the doors took forever to open.

Two minutes.

Neil tried to hurry, but the best he could do was a waddle, and his lungs were already on fire, not to mention his legs.

For a moment he wished he was back in the game. He didn't have to worry about lugging himself down that way.

He reached the door to their space a few seconds later, sweat trickling down his brow.

Less than thirty seconds to go, and a maze of cubicles to get through.

Most everyone else was already there with headsets on as he shuffled by.

He was going to make it.

Neil pushed harder, moving his legs as fast as they could go, feeling his body move.

Then, he was there, gasping for breath, and leaning on his cubicle wall.

"Blithe!" his boss shouted. Neil turned slowly, gasping for breath. His boss was scowling, tapping on his watch.

Which showed he was two minutes late.

4

TO THE SEA

Neil turned on the lights in his apartment, when he managed to push past the malfunctioning door, and threw in a microwave pizza.

He tore into a bag of chips while he was waiting, crunching them without any gusto.

He felt empty inside, and drained. Even though he didn't want them to, his thoughts wandered back to the shouting contest, which made him even more depressed.

All he wanted to do was escape, and he shut his eyes. He was on a beach in that daydream, and Veronica was sporting a hot pink bikini and slipping a straw between his lips, her body pressed up against his.

Those lips, those eyes. *That body.*

The microwave beeped.

Neil sighed, and opened his eyes, surrounded by his drab brown kitchen in his drab brown apartment.

The pizza was hot, at least, not necessarily the best, but he wolfed it down, the spicy pepperonis burning his tongue and liquid magma tomato sauce.

He opened up an energy drink too, and after drinking half of it and polishing off the whole back of chips, which he wasn't particularly proud of, pushed through the mess of his room and back to the console.

The happy blue glow welcomed him, and it chimed when he slipped it on, prompting him to continue where he left off.

Neil happily accepted, and was swept into the world of Castlebound Adventures.

"Welcome back, Neil." Mavaret was there, welcoming him.

Neil flexed, trying to get used to this avatar-like body. Instead of the shirt and pants, he had swapped into a set of bronze mail he had made himself, from ore he had dug from the mines.

"Any news?" Neil asked, testing the drag the heavier armor had on his body. It was tight around his midsection, but sized appropriately for his build.

Mavaret was silent, and when Neil looked at him he wondered why. His normally stone face was even more blank than normal, and something was clutched in his left hand.

"What is it?"

"News from the mainland." Neil's heart skipped a beat at his words, one part excitement at the mention of a new land, and one part sadness at leaving this place he had grown fond of. Mavaret cleared his throat. "Alas, I am too old for this. But..."

"What is it?" Neil asked, mouth dry.

Mavaret hesitated, but then proffered the small scrap of parchment. "Sent by pigeon this morning. Read it for yourself."

Neil took it, and tried to decipher the small writing, holding it close to his eyes. He finished, then looked up. "A dragon?"

"Yes," Mavaret said, his face drawn and tight. "Even now he terrorizes and plunders. The enemy of my youth, long since I thought he was dead he comes out of hiding to mock me."

"He's captured someone, who is it?"

"Orphelia, princess of Songbrook." Mavaret shook his head. "A wonderful child full of heart and life."

A small part of him was deflated at hearing that she was a child. Neil had almost expected something like this, and was wondering what she was like.

Was she as beautiful as Veronica?

"Why do they call on you, surely there is someone in the kingdom that can help?"

"Come with me," Mavaret said, turning and walking to the dining room. "This will take a while."

He poured two ales, then sat Neil down and told him more of his past, how he had fought the dragon and thought he had given it a mortal wound.

"The serpent fell into the pit he crawled out of, and I thought he was gone. Fool." Mavaret drank deep of his mug.

Neil took a sip of his, pleasantly surprised again at how well it tasted. This was a special batch, brewed by Farmer Bill from some of his best hops.

"And now it's come back."

"Yes. I should have gone into its lair and killed it once and for all, but I was wounded and..."

Neil leaned forward. "Maybe I can help?"

"You aren't ready,' Mavaret said softly. His eyes wandered to Neil's, and there was a strange tenderness in them, and for a second Neil forgot he was just a digital construct.

He had grown more than fond of Mavaret, and the man's pain was palpable.

"I've done everything you've asked, and run out of quests on this island. What else is there to do?"

"I cannot keep you here forever. I knew that." Mavaret studied him as the colors of the sunset splashed across the clouds behind him. The bugs buzzed and the birds chirped as a soft breeze brought the fragrance of the jungle flowers in the hall.

This is strange. Neil wondered if he had missed one of the tutorials. He had already advanced all his skills a few levels, from herbology to melee fighting.

And in the weekend he had off Neil had explored all of the island, updating his map that was stored in his Amulet of Erondis.

He pulled it out now, upgraded to silver from the mines and a woven chain of fiber. Silver had added the map, which he studied now.

It had all the familiar landmarks, but not a hint of a quest.

"How do I get off the island?" Neil asked, his voice carried on the breeze.

"That, I will show you tomorrow," Mavaret said, draining his mug. "But tonight, we must have a celebration in your honor, the great Lancelot is on his way."

The quest parchment came up, which Neil signed gratefully, and together they gathered the villagers and prepared a feast.

Neil couldn't help but feel off though. He had more than a sneaking suspicion it wasn't supposed to go this way, that Mavaret was supposed to give him a quest to fight the dragon and save the child princess.

Even so, he was captured in the festivities when they began, burning a bonfire high into the night sky.

"Come, let me show you the night sky," Mavaret said when the meal had been polished off and more drinking had begun. "Look over there."

Three stars in close proximity twinkled along his path. "Those are the three sisters. If ever you find yourself lost, just remember to look up and find them. They always point north, no matter where you are."

"Three sisters?"

"They were young once, and beautiful beyond all compare, but they were vain and proud." Mavaret shook his head. "They rejected many suitors from all the lands, each one competing against each other for the most powerful and handsome man.

"Then, one night they had a stranger come to visit them. "Please let me stay the night," begged the man in tattered clothing.

"They spoke to each other, none wanting to host the man, and then they dismissed him back into the night, not even giving him a coat to protect him from the cold or a scrap of bread to ward off his hunger.

"No sooner had he left when the doors were swept open and a handsome man with flashing eyes and thunder in his heart entered. Each sister desired him, and each rushed forward to invite him in.

"'You have treated me with no respect as a beggar, and now you will pay the consequence, for it was I who came begging for a place to stay.' The sisters were aghast, and protested, but the man refused to listen to them.

"He cast them up into the heavens, setting them as a guide to the defenseless and poor, proclaiming 'In life you used your beauty in vanity, now you will use your beauty for good.'"

A snap of the fire broke the spell Neil had been under. "Who was this man?"

"He has no name that mortals can speak." Mavaret smiled, then looked up into the stars. "Besides, it is only an old tale. But remember the sisters if every you need guidance and are lost. They will direct you if you need it."

Neil followed his gaze. The sky was clear and cloudless, and a million stars sprinkled it like pixie dust. The crack of the bonfire and the sweet smelling smoke it made rose into the air.

"What is it about me that you don't want to tell me?" Mavaret didn't respond. "Is this because of my mark?"

"No, it's..." Mavaret looked to the side. "I don't have the heart to tell you now. You will know in time. Now it is late, and I must go." Mavaret rose and saluted him. "Goodnight Lancelot, and good luck."

Neil murmured back, "Goodnight." He too, rose, and went back to his own room, less bare than it had been. Mementos of his time learning on the island. He wondered if he could take them with him, or if they would be left.

It all seemed surreal. Neil sat on the bed, then laid down. The request to advance time hovered over him and he reached out.

His finger hovered over the morning, but something was holding him back. Was it the news that had come, was it Mavaret's holding back something he should have revealed?

Neil wouldn't find out tonight, so he pressed it and waited as time shifted around his head. The darkness left, and the morning sun streamed through the window a second later.

If only this could happen in real life. Neil felt a twinge of... something. He wasn't sure what.

He collected his things, put them in his bag, and gave his temporary home one last look. It had only been a weekend, but he already knew he was going to miss this place. Somehow it was more welcoming than anyplace he had stayed.

When he arrived at the beach, Mavaret was waiting for him. They exchanged pleasantries, then Mavaret motioned down the sparkling white sand.

"A boat?"

"Yes, it will take you to the mainland, and you will need this as well." Mavaret held out a scroll. Neil took it, and it hovered and disappeared in a blaze of light, sucking into his amulet. It went cold for a second, then projected the map, which updated and zoomed out.

"Your destination is Peak's End, just off the coast of Lagartia." The spot flashed on his map, and Neil studied it, tracking the distance between it and where they were. The island looked like a smudge in comparison to the continent that lay in front of him.

"And one last lesson to learn."

"Lesson?" Neil asked, furrowing his brow and putting aside the map. The light sucked back into his amulet.

"Yes," Mavaret said, smirking. "Seamanship."

How an old knight knew how to sail, Neil couldn't fathom, but Mavaret seemed adept and adroit at teaching it, even able to name knots and show him how to tie them.

He tried to tie the rough cords, thicker than any rope he had known, and scratchier too, but his hands were clumsy and he was only able to get the easiest.

"No matter," Mavaret laughed, as another slipped out of its loop into a limp coil. "There will be plenty of time to practice when we're out. Come." He motioned into the boat, and Neil stepped inside.

"Can I take everything with me?"

"It's yours to take," Mavaret said, and Neil climbed in. The old knight pushed the boat out into the surging waves, and then hopped in, somehow making his armor seem weightless.

A trick of the game, that must be it.

"Release the line," Mavaret said, pointing to the rope holding up the sail. Neil pulled at the end, just like he was told, and the sail came billowing down.

It caught the fresh, salty sea breeze and burst into full bloom. The boat leapt ahead in the onslaught, and Neil nearly fell over, but caught himself just in time.

Mavaret taught him more as they went, how to turn the small sailboat, and what to look for beneath the water to avoid.

"These waters are sprinkled with coral and rock that will slash a hole in a boat like this." Mavaret patted the side. "One of the reasons this island is so safe, but I'll show you the way through."

He guided it deftly through patches of dark, rock just lurking beneath the rolling waves. Neil licked his lips, tasting the salt of the foam, and let the sun beat down on his face.

It was a glorious moment, but as he looked back some of the joy faded.

Something about him hated leaving, and something even deeper inside him told him he wouldn't ever see the place again.

He hoped it was a lie, but he couldn't shake the feeling.

5

PEAK'S END

"Look up ahead." Mavaret nodded ahead of them.

There was a dark cloud on the horizon, laden with black and flashing with occasional streaks of lightning. A curtain of rain fell from it. "That looks bad."

"We can avoid it, if you catch it early enough. We'll go upwind and try and swing around if we can. Here we go." Mavaret worked the tiller, easing the boat to the left.

The cloud was moving, and the head of the boat pointed over and around it. Neil watched in fascination as the boat skimmed along, the rain cloud staying just off to their right.

It came close though, close enough for the thunder to roll off in waves. The air chilled.

An hour or so later and the deep blue water of the ocean shimmered in the distance up ahead. Neil squinted, staring hard at the horizon. It looked... brown.

He blinked, thinking the sun had dazzled him as it reflected off the waves. But, there it was.

"It's land," Mavaret said. "The mainland of Lagartia."

"How far away is it?"

"Another few hours with this wind." Mavaret pointed a little to the right of where they were headed. "That way lies the port city of Peak's End."

Neil was about to ask him when he was going to be able to see it when something jarred the boat and knocked him down off his perch on the side.

"What was that?" Neil asked, scrambling back to his feet in the bottom of the hull.

Mavaret had his hand on the tiller, but his other was wrapped around the handle of his sword.

Something hit the boat again. "Get my bow," Mavaret said, eyes following something outside the boat.

Getting back to his feet again, Neil rushed over to the small chest they had stored all their rations and equipment, other than what he had on him. It creaked open, and he grabbed the bow and arrows.

"Brace yourself," Mavaret said calmly. Neil grabbed onto the hull, and just in time.

This time, whatever hit the boat had built up enough speed that it made the boat veer off course.

But since he was ready for it, Neil was able to recover quickly and was at Mavaret's side a few seconds later.

"What is it?" he asked, out of breath.

Mavaret took the bow and knocked an arrow, drawing it to the right of the ship. As he let loose Neil saw what he was shooting at.

And his breath caught in his throat.

It was the biggest shark he had ever seen in his life. Its fin was cut and scraped, with a chunk missing out of the back.

Plumes of water flooded off of each side, forming sparkling cones that slipped into the sea and broke up the white surf.

Twang. The arrow flew straight and true, striking just below the waterline of the fin.

It hit, and the thing flinched, then pulled up out of the water with a roar that echoed across the short distance.

Neil pulled back reflexively, and almost covered his ears it was so loud. When it was done, and u the momentary glimpses of horrendous mouth and jagged rows of teeth was gone, along with that chilling yellow eye, he realized how much danger they were in.

But Mavaret was still knocking arrows and taking aim. More flew, slipping into the sea with a whistle and barely a splash.

"Hold the tiller, bring us to the left." Mavaret was grim faced, but perfectly calm.

Neil was trying to keep hold of himself, even though he knew this was a game. A fetid smell had risen from the monster's direction, overpowering the salt and fresh air of the sea.

"Why is it doing this?" Neil grabbed for the warm, smooth wood of the tiller handle. After three attempts he managed it.

Mavaret spared him a glance between arrows. "The world is full of more than light and beauty. Shadows and evil hold fast just as easily. Turn now." Mavaret dropped his bow and swung into the rigging, pulling on the boom and shifting the sails.

Neil pushed on the tiller, even though he knew it was in the same direction as the monster shark. It was close, too close, and Neil braced himself.

Feet thumped across the wooden frame and the slick sound of a sword broke free of the scabbard.

Jaws, dripping water, opened to devour them.

With a flash of light and a shout Mavaret moved like lightning, far faster than any man Neil had seen.

The shark ripped in two, splaying open for a moment before it shimmered and shone. It fell back into the sea in a torrent, water splashing and rolling over the short deck of the boat.

"Straighten her," Mavaret said, pulling a hook from inside the keel of the boat. He slammed it into the now floating body of the shark and hauled it up and into the boat.

Neil's eyes widened when the entire boat sunk down at least two feet deeper, and he was amazed at both Mavaret's strength and the size of the monster.

While they approached the mainland Mavaret dug into the flesh, scraping it away with his knife, and rummaging around inside.

"As I suspected." Mavaret's hand closed around something, then he pulled it out. It glittered in the afternoon sun.

"What is it?"

"Its powershard. Corrupted too." A pale green riddled the surface of the blazing red gem.

"What's a powershard?"

"It's the essence of a monster, what gives it power. One of the surest ways of killing them is to find it and break it, but it isn't the only way." Mavaret walked back and took control of the tiller.

"Why would it attack us?" Neil stared at the beast, the foul odor he had smelled before coming from it. It ruined an otherwise good experience.

"I don't know." Mavaret stared at the horizon, at something Neil couldn't see. The land was bigger, more pronounced, and less brown. It had a touch of green to it. Vegetation, or trees, Neil couldn't tell yet. "But whatever drove it was powerful evil."

Even Neil could sense it, rolling off the dead carcass in waves. What it was though...

"It's unsettling." Neil turned away from it. "Can we get rid of it?"

"There is value in the meat and hide. It can be sold for good coin in Peak's End. You can cut it up while I sail."

Neil frowned, but rose to his feet and approached the thing. Its pale eye stared unceasingly at him. The thought of putting his hand into its flesh, the blood that would come out.

It was too much.

"I can't do it."

"Nonsense," Mavaret said. "You've dressed smaller animals before."

"Yes, but those were chickens and we were going to eat them."

"We can eat it. I don't know how good it will taste."

The thought of that strange, rubbery skin in his mouth almost made Neil vomit. *It's just a game.* He had to remind himself a few more times before the thought went away.

"I'd rather not."

Mavaret shrugged. "Suit yourself. Take the tiller."

Neil couldn't help notice the disappointment in his eyes, and his cheeks burned with shame as he sat to steer.

With a clean, and sharp, knife Mavaret made short work of the shark, piling the meat neatly on one side and the skin and... everything else, on the other.

"Take this." Mavaret held out the powershard, clean now but still riddled with the strange green substance.

It was cool, almost cold, to the touch. Neil turned it over, studying its surface. "What can you do with them?"

"Some merchants buy them, some crafters can use them in their craft. Others collect the finest specimens, and pay the most for them." Mavaret sat down beside him and took the tiller.

"It all seems so strange to me. The island, the letter, and now this?"

Mavaret glanced at him. "Yes. We live in strange times. The world is not what it used to be."

Neil slipped the gem into his pouch, patting it lightly. When he was out of the game he might look them up, if he could. The net was strangely silent about the game, still waiting for the wider release this Friday.

The rest of the journey passed quickly, and soon they were sliding into dock, a helpful sailor on the other end to catch the rope.

Neil was too busy watching the activity around him.

Boats of every size sailed around them, large barks, small schooners, rowboats. Their paddles beat the calm water and their voices sailed out over the distance between them. Laughter, jests, and a few names were called.

It mixed with the merchants and hustle and bustle of the docks. Large, barrel chested men carried equally impressive casks down gangplanks of the large vessels. Merchants called out, hawking their wares.

Mavaret gently pushed Neil, who was so taken in by the smells of cooking meat, salt air, spices, and filth, that he hadn't realized how much he was staring.

"Time to get off, and into the city."

"Right," Neil said, standing up and crossing the short plank to the dark brown dock covered with barnacles below the waterline.

Once back on dry land, or rather the rocking and creaking wood, Neil was at a loss as to what to do next.

He turned back and found Mavaret still in the boat.

"Are you coming?"

"No," he said softly. "This land is yours to discover, and yours to protect." Something troubled him behind his stern eyes, but he reached into his purse and covered up his... discomfort?

Neil wasn't sure what to make of it when he handed him a small scroll. "I know you have questions, and some of them I have no right to not answer. I hope you'll forgive me, when you find out why."

His mouth was dry, and his throat scratchy, but Neil managed to keep it calm. "What is this?"

"A quest, if you choose to take it." Mavaret nodded to the sailor, who spit a wad of something dark brown out of his mouth into the water and began untying the rope that held Mavaret's boat.

"Thank you, for everything," Neil said. The words were as hollow as he felt. *He's just a character in a game. Why are you feeling like this?*

"Good luck Lancelot. May the sun never set on you." Mavaret raised his hand as the sailor pushed the bow of his boat away from the pier and around to the ocean. The calls of seagulls crying in the air seemed to be mocking him and the softness that was coming to Neil's eyes.

Neil tried to blink it away, watching Mavaret's sails puff up with wind and take him away. He stood, surrounded by the hustle and bustle of the docks, as it receded into the cool, blue line of the horizon.

He clutched the leather scroll in his hand, breathing the sea air. He was alone again. Truly, and well, alone.

6

GARDEN OF TRANQUILITY

The port city of Peak's End spread out like a pool of water around the harbor. Neil found himself nearly in the center of it, but instead of a calm, clear pool, it was a raging flood of movement, sounds, and smells that reminded him of the city.

And the thought brought him back to the real world, for a moment.

Neil swallowed and pulled up his map. Much of it was unrevealed, other than the small circle that surrounded him, and didn't help much. For some reason he didn't want to read the scroll Mavaret had given him, so he slipped it into his small pouch that held his coins, and took stock of his surroundings.

The wooden pier he was on led onto a rough cobblestone road right next to a pile of boulders and rocks that the waves slapped up against. Most of the movement and action was here, and into it he knew he had to go.

Shops, buildings, and warehouses lined the side opposite the water. Some looked brand new, others dilapidated and at the verge of falling down.

What to do. With his stats low, Neil knew he had to train up somehow, but there was so much to do and see he didn't know where to start.

So Neil walked down the pier, observing everything around him as he did. The rush of people was almost overwhelming in the street, and he had to wait as a few carts filled with goods rumbled by before he could cross to the side with the buildings.

When they were past he looked for an opening, rushing into a gap, but he was swept away with the crowd to the right. All along the street merchants were yelling out, trying to get his, or anyone who would listen, attention.

"Clothing, silk from the east as soft and smooth as a baby's bottom. Come inside and feel," said a man in fine clothing, ruffles and decorations all over him like a peacock, and a smile like oil. His eyes fixed on Neil. "Come, sir, come see the wares to replace those rags and send you out in style." He beckoned with a hand filled with rings that clinked together.

Trying to avoid his gaze, Neil tried to push deeper into the crowd, narrowly avoiding the man's grasp. Men and women surrounded him, carrying him downstream in a crushing press of bodies.

Neil couldn't do anything but follow along, and found himself helpless. Buildings passed by like trees on the banks of a river. He pushed, trying to get out of the rush.

Finally, he pushed through the last layer of people, and he was out, deposited into an alley. He stood gasping, wondering at the strength that had been drained from the quick trip. There was no sight of the small pier he had come from, in fact he was almost out of the docks and into the heart of the city.

A cat screamed behind him, and Neil started. He whirled, just in time to see it scramble up the side of the wall and scattering a pile of trash in a clatter.

A sniff brought the stench of old garbage that had rotted in the sun, and Neil covered his nose, eyes watering. The alley was filled with trash, boxes, and refuse. It ended in a brick wall missing one or two.

When he turned back to the street there was a small child standing in front of him.

Neil almost jumped again, heart racing. He wasn't sure why, but the child's sudden appearance unsettled him.

"Please sir, have you seen my cat?" the young boy asked, voice quavering and thin, almost as thin as the arms and legs that more resembled sticks than human appendages.

"Cat?" Neil looked back. "I saw a cat over there. What color was it?"

"Black, and big."

Neil tried to remember what color the cat had been, but he had only caught a glimpse. The young boy's eyes were so plaintive and filled with emotion he couldn't look away.

"I... don't know. It had only been a second."

"Oh." The boy's face fell. "Sorry to bother you."

The boy turned back to the street, but something wasn't right. "Do you... want help?"

"Oh yes." The boy whirled around, clapping his hands with joy. "Do you promise?"

A quest sheet materialized, written in a child's scratchings: The Boy's Cat.

With a smile, Neil signed it and it rolled up and disappeared. "I can help with that. And after, you might help me find my way around this city."

"I can show you everywhere!" The boy was happy now, face filled with cheer. Neil pulled out a loaf of bread and offered it, and the boy's eyes shone even brighter as he pounced on it.

"What's your name?"

"Tad," the boy said between bites. Neil introduced himself as Lancelot, getting the pleasantries out of the way.

"Where do you think your cat is?"

"Dunnno. He runs away sometimes." Bits of bread flew out of Tad's mouth, and Neil backed up a step. He wondered where this boy had come from, and if he shouldn't be doing something else, but he looked like he needed help and Neil couldn't bear to see him go away empty handed.

"Let's try the other side of this wall then." Neil looked back to the wall, trying to see if there was any way to get over it.

It looked damaged, crumbling, and even with bricks missing there weren't enough hand-holds to get up the seven or eight feet to the top.

Neil looked through one of the holes. The other side wasn't an alley.

He drew back in surprise, then had to take another look, and confirmed it.

There was a garden on the other side of the wall. Flowers bloomed in well-laid beds, with a carpet of green grass in between. A medium-sized tree grew in the center, adorned with a kind of fruit Neil had never seen before.

"There's a garden over there," Neil said. Then, he saw it. A black cat lounged in the branches of the tree, tail flicking back and forth. "Is that your cat?"

Tad pressed his eye to the hole. "That's him! You've found him!" He danced with excitement. "Come on, Bruiser, come here."

"Is he coming?"

"No, he's just sitting there. We're going to have to go get him."

Neil looked up, around, to both sides, but couldn't find any entrance. "Do you know how he got there?"

Tad shook his head. "No, but we've got to get him. He's all alone in there and sad."

Sure doesn't look sad to me. Neil pulled up his map, trying to see if there was a way around. There was a vague outline of houses, but it was covered in the foggy gray of everything he hadn't explored yet.

"It looks like we can go around. Come on." Neil was eager to get out of the alleyway, both for the horrible smells of trash and human feces that was rotting in the sun, and the precarious nature of the surrounding buildings that were one push away from falling over.

The crowd had thinned some since he had been ejected from it, but it was still a press of bodies.

Neil hesitated, but Tad pushed out into the crowd, pulling him by the hand. He couldn't help but follow, flowing with the crowd down to the intersection, and shoving his way through to the less traveled side street.

According to the map this would take them down perpendicular to the garden, and they would have to go down an alleyway to the left.

"Over here," Neil said, pulling Tad into a larger alley and down a more respectable looking street. The houses here looked solid, if a bit worse for wear, and flanked the streets like two story soldiers of brown stone.

The map led him just opposite the alley they had been in, and brought them to the front door of a stern, brown faced building two stories tall.

Windows, black and blocked, leered at the. Neil couldn't shake the feeling of being watched.

"This is... it?" Neil scratched his head, the garden had been beautiful and well-tended. This house looked run down at best, and dilapidated from years of neglect. He wasn't sure the brown brick that made up its front would stay attached.

Tad kept behind him, clutching at his shirt. It couldn't be helped, so Neil stepped up, heart pounding, and knocked at the big black door.

He held his breath, half expecting something to jump out at him, but a hand on the door and the clacking of a lock shifting soon allowed the upper half of the door to swing open.

"Who is it?" boomed a voice, coming from a thick, balding man covered in scars. His beady black eyes glared at Neil and Tad.

Neil opened his mouth, which had gone dry and cottony, and struggled to search for the words.

"Out with it, before I beat it out of you." The man didn't sound like he was joking.

"We're looking for a cat," Neil stammered.

The man's eyes narrowed. The room inside was bright, and laughter from somewhere deeper in the house drifted out.

"Come back here again and I'll kill you." The man slammed the door shut, which made Neil jump. The echo of it rang through the street.

Well that's that. Neil turned, resigned to the end of his quest.

"Please sir," Tad said, his eyes wide and pleading. His face was contorted and twisted, and his hands clutched together in a prayer. "He's all alone out there, and so scared."

His eyes returned to the door, large and ominous, then back to Tad's eyes.

How am I supposed to help him?

Neil looked around, trying to think at the same time. He studied the wall, and looked to the top. He swallowed. It was tall, too tall to climb.

The houses to each side butted up against it, tight to either wall, nowhere to squeeze by or up against.

And still, Tad kept looking at him. Neil shifted from foot to foot, then did the only thing he could think of.

With a few quick movements, he logged out.

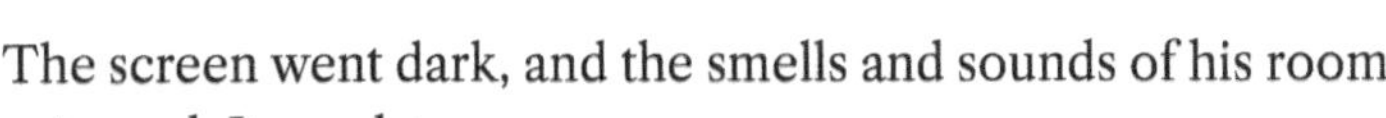

The screen went dark, and the smells and sounds of his room returned. It was late.

Too late.

The clock flashed 2:34 a.m.

Even if he went to bed now he wouldn't be able to get enough sleep. Neil returned the console to its charger. It chimed gently, then blinked green.

The look in Tad's eyes lingered on his mind, and he felt sick to his stomach. Neil closed his eyes, and put his hands over them, trying to block out the sight.

But it was no good.

He scrambled up out of his bed, crossing the dirty room to the refrigerator, and popped open a soda and downed it in a few gulps. A bag of chips chased it, and it helped.

Neil sat in the glow of the refrigerator, but no matter what he tried to think about he couldn't get Tad's eyes out of his mind.

7

PROBATION

The alarm blared, sucking Neil from his dream. In some measures he was glad to get out of the strange dream, where he had been stuck in a pool of what felt like sticky jelly. No matter which way he turned it held him fast, pulling him back under.

He rubbed his bloodshot eyes and dressed as quickly as he could, but his body dragged more than usual. It was already fifteen minutes past eight when he got out the door, not enough time to stop by the bakery for his usual pack of donuts for breakfast.

He hurried to the train station, but it was running behind.

Of course. Can anything in my life go right for a change? By the time the next one came in the station was bursting at the seams, and there was barely enough room for him to get on, let alone sit, so he sweated near a window, grateful for the view at the very least.

Neil had to run the rest of the way to the office and was out of breath after the first block. He managed to get to his desk with two minutes to spare though, with Goltan glaring at him through his window.

The look made his skin crawl, and it told him everything he needed to know. Another screw up and he'd be gone, another job down the drain.

Would it really be that bad, though? Neil pushed the thought aside and started answering calls.

The first one didn't go that bad, he helped a lady through a tough time with her modem, and the next was fine too. His metrics were green, no flashing warning signs or red to speak of.

The third call, however, didn't go quite as well. The man had a thick accent, and it was hard for Neil to decipher.

"Did you say cheeseburger?" Neil asked, cringing as soon as the word came out. *Why would anyone be calling about a cheeseburger?*

"No, surge protector," the man said, slowly enunciating his words.

"Oh, surge protector. I can help you with that right away."

But he couldn't help him with it, and he wasn't sure what a surge protector had to do with their net system. By the time he had escalated the issue up his screen was flashing yellow.

Over by fifteen minutes, just to get the basic information recorded. It had taken the man three tries just to get his phone number right, and Neil still wasn't convinced he had the right number.

"Neil, in my office now," Goltan said, somehow appearing over his cubicle wall. Neil jumped, heart pounding, and wiped his sweaty hands on his pants.

Which he had forgotten to change, in his rush out the door. The mustard stain from lunch was still there in his crotch.

Neil groaned. Now he was going to get a talking to and look like a fool at the same time. He wanted to crawl into a hole and die.

Shoulders slumped, and listening to the tittering and gossip from his co-worker's cubicles, Neil slunk back to Goltan's office.

⸻◆○◆⸻

"Another talking to?" Bob asked, sitting down across from Neil, whose tray was loaded up with three kinds of dessert.

"I don't want to talk about." Neil pushed his mashed potatoes around with a fork, then took a clump of them and ate it. They smelled like cafeteria potatoes, and tasted just as bland, but even a little salt and a heaping helping of butter didn't help.

"Sorry to hear that. How's the game going?"

Neil had almost forgotten about that, but then Tad's look came rushing back. The look of pleading, of utter despair, and all he ignored with one click of a button.

He isn't real, Neil.

"Fine."

"That's it? Jeez, it must really have been bad." Bob's eyes were wide with surprise.

"I'm on probation. One more screw up and I'm toast." Neil chewed an obligatory mouthful of burger and washed it down with a deep gulp of soda. The food helped, he was feeling a little better.

But he knew it would wear off in an hour, or two if he was lucky. And then he'd be back to fat Neil, a worthless coward who couldn't even help a little boy find a cat.

"I'm not going to last the week."

"Don't think like that, you've been in pinches before. Everyone has their slumps."

"This isn't a slump, and I've never officially been on probation before. The Devil was practically wringing his hands as I read it, and probably wanted me to sign it in blood. I swear he's some kind of demon."

"A balding demon, maybe." The thought of it brought a hint of a smile to Neil's face, and then a chuckle. "See, it isn't all bad, we can always draw Goltan like he's supposed to be."

"Can you imagine the look on his face if we plastered it all over the office?" Neil wore a full smile now, and continued, "He wouldn't live it down ever."

"That would be good. See," Bob said. "You're looking on the right side now."

"Thanks, man. I needed that right about now."

"No problem." Bob reached out a hand. "You know how it is, when we go, we go all the way for each other."

Neil brushed off the majority of the grease from his, and encased Bob's hand in large sausage-like fingers. "You know it."

Bob dug into his food as Neil ran him through the troubles and the failed quest in his game. "As soon as it comes out you have to get a copy, you're going to love it."

"It's another two weeks, I don't know if I can wait that long. Besides, my mom is really up in me for failing prep right now."

"Did you tell her you did it on purpose?" Neil asked, with a grin.

"Not in a million years," Bob said, his lips drawn into a grimace. "And don't you even think about telling her."

"When am I going to see her?"

"When you come over and we play together, that's when."

"Oh, I forgot." Most of the mirth evaporated, leaving a grim atmosphere over the two. "How has it been since...?"

"The hours are tough, and I still can't make enough. I wish I had found a killer steal like your pad."

"It comes with its disadvantages." Neil stirred up his potatoes again. Were they taking on a distinct yellow hue? "Like all the crime, and the noise. Last night it took me forever to get to bed, someone was fighting just down the hall."

"So it's the noise that kept you up, and not Castlebound Adventures?" Bob asked, one eyebrow raised.

Neil shrugged. Someone dropped a tray, silverware clattering everywhere, and it distracted him for enough time to forget about it.

They talked and finished lunch before the bell rang. Neil wished he could stay longer, somewhere other than the oppressive cubicle that seemed to be getting smaller every day.

The cafeteria had light from the windows, a bright spot in his day, unlike the dungeon floor he worked in. Up there the florescent lights gave him a headache, making him miserable.

It was all he could think about as he trudged to the elevator, joining the long line of silent passengers until it was his turn to board. He squeezed into the corner, self-conscious of how much room he took up, and wished he was smaller, like Bob. He didn't have problems taking up too much room.

As the elevator doors opened, Neil felt an oppressive weight descend on him. Goltan watched him go to his cubicle. There was nothing he would enjoy more than firing Neil, and Neil hated him for it.

Why can't he leave me alone? I haven't done anything to him. But Neil knew he wouldn't leave him alone.

He was going to make his life miserable.

Neil sat into his hard, almost broken chair, and put on the horribly fitting headset. He closed his eyes and wished the day was over.

8

POSTED: RAT INFESTATION

Neil sat in his apartment, wondering what he would do. The console was warm in his hands, and a faint tingling ran through it where the electronics hummed. All it would take was one little motion and he could be back in the game.

But was it an escape? How could he face those eyes, that accusing look?

"There must be something else I can do. Mavaret taught me to fight, I might as well try to cut my way through. *Besides, what's the worst that could happen?*

So he slipped the strap over the back of his head, the transmit module settling right at the base of his skull, and laid back in his soft bed.

The ceiling of his room, with that strange shaped water stain that always seemed like a lion to him, dissolved into Castlebound Adventures.

And Tad was right there in front of him, waiting like a sad puppy dog.

"Don't worry kid, we'll get your cat," he said, more confidently than he felt. *It's just a game.*

He closed his gloved hand around the hilt of his short sword, and checked to see how his health was. Full, and with a few health potions to spare. Whatever would happen next, he was ready for it.

He wished he had some of the higher-level enchantments on his equipment, or even stronger weapons, but a few more hours playing would help with that.

And finishing this quest was sure to give him some kind of reward.

"Thank you!" Tad was ecstatic, and clutched at his arm while he jumped up and down. It made Neil feel better, and gave him a bit more confidence as he went back to the door.

With a drawn sword he pounded on it. "Let us in, we need to get back to your garden."

He stood back, prepared to fight, as the thump of the big man's feet sounded behind the door. Locks were thrown, and clicks sounded, until the man opened the door, scowling at the interruption.

"I said if you came back I'd kill you. You'll regret this." He pulled an enormous, two-handed sword from behind the door and advanced.

Neil regretted his decision as soon as the big man swung. That mass of metal came at his head faster than he expected, or wanted, and he barely had time to get his sword up to parry it.

The second hit slashed across his shoulder. Pain seared up Neil's arm, and he cried out involuntarily.

The big man only grinned.

Neil fell back, downing a health potion, and feeling relief flood into his system. His eyes were watering, and the taste of iron flooded his mouth.

"I told you I'd kill you," the man said, licking his lips and advancing.

Neil didn't want to fight anymore, and looked around for a way out. His eyes fell on Tad, who was depending on him.

I can't. But that look...

How was he going to get away without leaving Tad?

"Get out of here," Neil said, gritting his teeth as the blow from his parry shuddered down his arm. "Go."

"No, I'm not leaving you," Tad said.

Neil's heart sank. The man's huge sword flashed, drawing a deep gash down his thigh. Blood poured out of him, the scent of it filling the air.

He reached for another portion, but the man came on like a whirlwind. Everyone Neil tried to escape, he was there.

I need to attack.

But there was no good opening for it. Neil realized that he wasn't fast, he was overwhelmed with trying to keep up.

And it wasn't working. Another gash was drawn down Neil's torso.

The attacks kept coming. Neil tried to thrust forward, going for the man's belly, but with a laugh the man brushed it aside.

"Pitiful. It's time to end this." The man's eyes narrowed, and he swung the two-handed sword with more power.

Neil's small blade was like a leaf before the wind. Another smash sent it spinning out of his hands, leaving him defenseless.

Something slipped into his gut. Cold, hard. The pain came after.

Neil looked down. It was the blade. His heart pounded, slowing as his broken body bled.

He couldn't believe it. The world went dark.

The game menu appeared.

Neil felt like he was floating in nothingness. He looked around, above, below, behind him, but there was nothing but that glowing menu in front of him.

Continue from your last save point?

Save point? When was the last time I saved? He thought back. It had to be when he logged out last.

Right before the fight.

He thought about turning the game off, going to get something to eat, but then he kept thinking about Tad and the look in his eyes.

Tad needed him. He needed someone to look out for him.

Neil remembered what that was like, knew it even today. He couldn't let that happen.

He pushed aside thoughts of eating, and reached out and touched the continue button.

The menu winked out of existence, and the alley materialized around him. Tad was still there, waiting and watching with those sad eyes.

"I... I can't help you right now," Neil said, heart wrenching, "but I'll come back, I promise."

"You promise?" Tad asked, his face steeling. Neil nodded.

"I have to get stronger. When I'm stronger..." Neil reached out and ruffled Tad's hair. It was soft, but ratty with years of neglect.

With a sad smile Neil turned away and walked back to the main street. He wasn't sure where Tad would go, or where he would find him next, but he had to work on his levels.

Neil stepped back from the main street and into an alcove beside a bakery, wonderful smells drifting from it, and brought up his stats.

The few days on the island had helped, but Neil didn't realize until he looked at it just how weak in his fighting skills he was. His bladed level was two, and that was just because he had done some training on the dummies Mavaret set up for him workouts, and his defense and armor ratings were still at one.

He had to find some low-level monsters to train on, but Mavaret hadn't given him any leads on that, and it was too early for anything to be out on the net.

Which meant he was on his own.

"Where would I go if I was weak and wanted to stay hidden?" Neil thought about it for a while, then pulled up the map.

It had a legend, and he searched through it to find something resembling a dungeon. There had to be something in the city, or close to it, and if this was the starting area the monsters inside should be relatively weak.

But most of his map was covered in gray fog, what he found was unexplored territory, and the little he had uncovered didn't have anything promising.

With a sigh Neil shut his menu. As he saw it he could either wander around aimlessly, or he could find an NPC that knew something.

And he wasn't sure wandering around was such a good idea, considering how he had fared with the thug.

So, Neil stared at the closest building, the bakery.

A bell above the door dinged as he entered.

"Welcome, traveler. How can I help you?" a portly woman asked, coming out from in the back wiping the flour dust off her hands on to her apron. Most of the front of her was covered in white.

Neil resisted looking at the rows of breads, cakes, and other baked goods spread out on the wooden shelves, and the mouthwatering smells they made.

"Good morning," Neil said, suddenly feeling awkward, "I'm looking for... monsters?"

"No monsters here, love," the woman said. "Just baked goods. Would you like to try some?" She picked up a loaf and offered it to him.

Neil held up his hands. "No, no. I'm sorry, I was just looking for somewhere to train."

"Ah, an adventurer."

"Er, yes."

"The post board would be a good place to start." Her eyes were warm, and twinkled, which helped to relax him.

"What's that?"

"It's a place in the main square where anyone can request help from adventures, for an adequate reward of course. I used it to get rid of a nasty rat infestation last year." She raised an eyebrow, noticing him staring at the bread. "Are you sure you don't want a taste? It's good."

Neil licked his lips. "Well...why not?"

\#

He felt guilty taking the loaf, until he bit into it. It was warm and fluffy, with a nice crunch on the outside just like a chip.

How do they get the taste? Does it come from the olfactory chip? Neil wasn't sure, but devoured it nonetheless.

It was beyond delicious. After a few moments of explanation from the baker on where the board could be found, and a quick exchange of funds for goods, Neil left the bakery a little bit poorer back out into the busy streets of Peak's End.

He licked the last of the crumbs off his fingers, still marveling at the taste, and tucked the rest of the baked goods into his pack.

Even though he had his map out while she was describing the way, he still got turned around a few times before he found the square.

It was big, far larger than the narrow streets that fed it, and had a fountain in the middle with a figure of a female riding on a swan that spouted water from its mouth. Wings were spread, detailed down to the feather, and the white rock reflected the light in a dazzling display of beauty.

Merchants were set up in colorful tent stalls all around the outside, yelling and talking and laughing as they sold their wares.

Peak's End was a hotbed of travel and trade. Most were dressed in simple garb of muted wool, but the travelers stood out in strange dress and mannerism.

Neil walked by them all, headed straight for the large board flanked by two stone knights with swords in hand outstretched to the sky. Nothing else captured his attention.

Parchments and bits of paper were plastered everywhere around the board, which was shielded from the rain by a large stone overhang. As Neil stepped into its shadow he also found it kept the sun out of his eyes too.

He scanned the board, reading the notices posted for adventurers, alone. Some described terrifying creatures terrorizing close by villages, others were merely pleased to get rid of small pests of monsters.

One of these simpler requests caught his eye, an echo from the baker perhaps, still stuck in his mind.

An unsteady hand had written out a small request, and Neil stepped closer to make out the words.

Adventurer, my farm is in need. Pleased kill the rats that are here.

No signatures, no name, only a simple map with an x scrawled on the back of it.

"Sounds simple enough." Neil plucked the paper from the board, and a quest contract appeared in mid-air. It was just as simple as the request, and Neil signed it.

As it was disappearing he noticed the figure looming off beside him on his right by the shadow that blocked out the sun on his back.

He almost jumped back when he caught a glance of the person casting it out of the corner of his eye.

It was a big, burly knight covered from head to toe in plate mail, but it wasn't any plate mail.

His armor was decorated in the form of demon faces and bodies, twisted all around his form, culminating in a helmet that sprouted twisted looking horns wreathed in flame.

As he looked on, Neil realized the flames were moving.

"Stand aside," a voice said, gravelly and deep, issued from inside the demonic helm.

Neil was quick to oblige, still clutching his mission. The knight reached up and took the most elaborate request, written on sheepskin parchment with gold ink, turned around, and strode off.

Who was that? The knight gave off a strange aura, in addition to the flames, that seemed to wreath him in strength. People stared at him as he walked, whispering behind his back when he had gone far enough to be out of earshot.

Neil wondered what kind of gear that was, and how he could get it. An image of himself in it came to his mind, then it was quickly dashed when he looked down at his belly.

He would never fit in that. Not in a million years.

His fist had crumpled the paper up, and he tried to relax to smooth it back out. It was all useless, all of it.

A few quick motions and he logged out. He was back in his apartment, the sun sinking outside. He blinked against the fading light and turned on his lights.

His room was dingy compared to the game, a mess of old clothes and trash that he hadn't cleaned up in weeks or months.

It made him feel worse, and he went to the kitchen to sate his hunger. The glow of the freezer revealed his stash of frozen meals, and he grabbed a bacon and sausage mac and cheese, then added a frozen pizza to it.

They were both covered in plastic that crinkled as he tore them open, the stale smell of frozen food unappetizing.

He remembered the taste of that bread, and thought about going out, but it was almost nine o'clock and none of the local bakeries would be open.

He wasn't even sure they would taste all that good. So, he put the mac and cheese in the microwave and the pizza in the oven, then leaned back against the counter to listen to the hum of the microwave.

He stared off into the distance, wondering how his life had become this. Other than the sound of the microwave, and the yelling of his neighbors, his apartment was quiet.

And the beeps as his mac and cheese finished only punctuated how alone he was.

He took the steaming plastic bowl from the microwave and dug into it. The macaroni was rubbery, but the meat was salty and good. He downed it before the pizza finished warming and sat at the edge of his bed.

What if I could be like that knight? Confident, strong, the envy of all around me?

Neil shook his head. He might be good at video games, but he would never be like that in real life.

9

The Beginner's Quest

The eating helped, and he devoured the pizza in a few minutes, then grabbed a soda for good measure.

The sugar went to his head right away, and he laid back in his bed to stare at the ceiling. It was almost 9:30 now. He knew he should go to bed soon, he had work in the morning, but he was feeling good enough and itched to go back into the game.

So he grabbed the console, put it on, and slipped back into Castlebound Adventures.

The market square was just as busy, and just as filled with sounds and smells. His heart gave a flutter. Neil looked around, but there was no sign of that knight.

It was back to the quest, to hopefully level up his skills more. He pulled up his map, now marked with a small dot where the quest start was to take place, well outside the walls of the castle.

In the game it was still afternoon, with plenty of light to spare. Time moved differently here, faster somehow, but he would have enough time to get out to do the quest.

If he started now. Neil turned and set out down the main street, heading in the general direction of the northern gate he thought he was supposed to go out.

The square ended at the houses, which flanked the streets like sentinels. In this part of the city they were well cared for, but they looked the same. A row of carefully constructed houses with windows and doors in all the same places.

It felt strange walking down the street, and he had a suspicion that he was being watched, but he never could catch sight of anyone staring at him.

The sounds of the market faded as he went along, replaced by the trundling of carts and the conversation of street travelers. Traffic was far lighter here than down at the docks, only a few gaggles of people going to and fro.

After a few wrong turns, with a quick retracing of his steps, he spotted the northern gate just up ahead as he rounded a curve.

Neil sighed and quickened his pace. He was losing time walking when he needed to be training. Tad's look kept haunting him.

Several soldiers stood sentry at the gate, primarily focused on those coming into the city, but a few keeping an eye out on the inner side. A line of hopeful entrants stretched out beyond, all waiting their turn as the guards stopped them for questioning.

Neil walked past, somehow nervous as a guard laid an eye on him. They were wearing shining half helmets, studded in a band around their forehead, which did nothing to hide their hard gazes.

The guard let him pass without a word though, and Neil breathed out as his legs tried to reconsolidate from the jelly they had been.

He wasn't used to so much walking, and realized that some of their weakness was from overuse. His breathing was labored too, as he huffed and puffed to go up the hill that led away from the city.

Neil stopped to catch his breath at the top, sitting down on the grass beside the dusty road. It was warm beneath his touch, although a bit rough when he moved his fingers across it.

He looked back towards the city and his throat caught in his breath. Peak's End was a jewel glittering on the coast. Beyond the hodgepodge collection of buildings the sea glimmered and shone as it reflected the strong afternoon sun.

"Beautiful." Neil was impressed with the graphics. Everything felt like it was real, from the dirt beneath his fingers to the smell of crushed grass. He looked closer at the ground, wondering if the illusion would break.

A small ant walked between stalks of grass. It was black and covered with small tufts. Its antenna moved like an ant would in the real world.

Neil's jaw dropped. That they would take the time to make even the ants so lifelike. *That's...incredible.*

Something didn't feel quite right about it, though. His mind kept telling him it was real, but this was all built by someone else. Someone who had programmed this world bit by bit, byte by byte.

How long had it taken them to do it? Neil glanced back up at the sky. It was starting to get late, and he was nervous about being caught outside the safety of the walls in the darkness. Who knew what kind of monsters roamed around at night?

He struggled back to his feet, feeling the tightness in his calves, and started back down the road after a quick check of the map.

It wasn't far now, just a few hundred yards or more away. A minute later he could see the farm. The farmhouse sat squat in a grouping of fields, with a larger, ill taken care of barn beyond.

But the marker took him here. He hurried the last few yards up the beaten path to the front door and knocked on it.

There was a small clattering inside, then the sound of a bolt being thrown and a crack appeared, harboring eyes inside.

"What do you want?" an old man's voice drifted through the opening.

"I'm here for the quest. Something about taking care of rats?" The eyes inside narrowed and looked him over.

"I put that up for an adventurer. Are you an adventurer?"

Neil's smile froze on his face. "Yes. I'm an adventurer. Lancelot's my name, it's a pleasure to meet you."

The man grunted, but he opened the door cautiously. Neil saw he had a pitchfork in his hand.

"Can't be too careful around here. We don't have walls to keep out the monsters like they do in the city." The man set the pitchfork up against the wall. "Come in."

Neil entered, ducking underneath the top of the doorway, and found another beam in his way with his head.

"Ow," he yelled, almost seeing stars from the blow.

"Mind your head. Name's Macgee."

Neil rubbed the front of his head, surprised that there wasn't a giant welt there, then realized it wouldn't do that in the game. *Or would it?*

The pain lingered, but it was manageable, and he followed the old farmer.

"Most of them are down here." Macgee pointed to a trap-door on the side of the kitchen, which was sparse and consisted of a fireplace, a few pots and pans, and a dilapidated chair and table. "That's where I keep my veg'bles. Confounded things keep eating everything in sight."

"How do they get in?" Neil avoided another low beam, eying it as he ducked under. The room smelled like dirt and smoke, with a strange leafy smell he couldn't quite put his fingers on underneath all of it. Neil sniffed again. It was almost like a mushroom, but not quite.

"Dug a tunnel right under the wall. Too scared to go through it, have to keep my veg'bles up in the attic for now." Macgee shook his head sadly. "Can't do it much longer, what with summer coming."

Neil raised an eyebrow. *What season is it here?* "I'll take a look."

"Best take this then." Macgee grabbed a stick sitting beside the fireplace, then lit it. It flamed up and Neil took the torch.

"Why?"

"It's dark down there in the tunnels." Macgee was stern and solemn. "Good luck boy."

"Thanks." Neil grabbed the iron ring of the trapdoor, cold beneath his fingers, and pulled it open with a wrenching creak. Rough rungs of a ladder descended into darkness, and after Neil held the torch down, right to the dirt floor beneath.

There was the tunnel opening, on the far side. It didn't look small at all, it was almost big enough for Neil to stand up in. He swallowed, then remembered that Tad was depending on him, and maybe others, and screwed up his courage.

He had to go down with his back to the opening, and since he had a torch already he couldn't draw his sword, which he longed to do. Neil took a deep breath, turned, and went down as quickly as he could while keeping his balance.

The temperature dropped a few degrees. His foot hit dirt and he spun, fumbling with the hilt of his sword.

He expected to see a swarm of rats, with fangs dripping blood, but there was only an empty hole and the empty cellar shelves. Scraps of discarded food were tucked into the corner, evidence of their attack on the farmer's goods.

"See them?" Macgee asked, face poking over the edge of the ladder, corners of his eyes wrinkled with concern.

"No." His heart was rushing, so Neil tried to calm down. He freed his sword and drew it, the rasp echoing in the small space. It made him feel better having it in his hand. "Just a bunch of rats," he said under his breath.

"What was that?"

"I'm going in," Neil said a little louder. Macgee said nothing.

Holding the torch out in front of him, Neil advanced into the hole.

He had to crouch down to fit through. As he entered the walls muted his footsteps. There were claw marks on the wall, bigger than any rat he had ever seen, not that he had ever seen any in real life.

But they were big enough for him to check the grip on his sword. *Was that a squeak?*

He stopped, holding his breath, ears straining in the darkness. The walls were tight here. *Will I even be able to swing my sword?*

Luckily, it was a short sword, not a two-handed monstrosity like the thug that had already killed him once.

Neil wiped a bead of sweat off his forehead and continued forward. There were no sounds at all in the earth.

The hairs on the back of his neck were standing up, and he felt eyes on his back. Neil whirled, flashing the torch in front of him.

Nothing.

He turned back, breath short and ragged. Stooping over was starting to hurt. The walls looked like they had narrowed at this point, but he wasn't sure.

Neil swallowed, held his sword out in front of him, and kept shuffling.

The tunnel seemed to stretch for miles. He felt like he'd been crouched down for hours. Then, the tunnel did get narrower, and he was forced to continue on hands and knees.

But a few more feet ahead it turned to the left, obstructing his view. Neil bit his lip. *How am I going to see?* Neil stopped to catch his breath.

And heard it.

Squeaking and scratching. It bored into his ears in the quiet tunnel, overriding the sound of his own breathing and heartbeat.

They were up there, waiting for him. Or ready to attack.

It isn't real, it's just a game. But it didn't feel like a game.

He adjusted the grip on his sword, and scuffled forward. Tad's eyes, his desperation, drove him forward. He couldn't help him without getting stronger.

He was at the edge of the turn now, and able to stand up in a crouch.

Neil took a deep breath, then charged around the corner.

The sharp turn took him into the opening of a cave, and he stuttered to a stop. He was able to stand here, glad to have a chance to stretch his back, but the smell was bad.

And then he saw the eyes.

Red, numerous, they reflected the light of the torch. And then the rats screamed at him and rushed to attack.

Neil jumped back in surprise, swinging his sword wildly. It was in vain, because the rats hadn't even entered the radius of his torchlight.

His back bumped against the side of the cave, hard and unyielding. Neil took a deep breath, remembering the advice Mavaret had given him.

"When you're in the heat of battle, take control of your body by breath."

So Neil breathed, sucking in a rotten smell of the cave and holding it.

And then the rats were upon him.

The first one entered the light of the torch. Its gray fur was mottled and clumped, missing in one patch behind its ear. Two sharp front teeth leered at him as it hissed and lunged.

As if by instinct, Neil brought up his sword. The rat impaled upon it, the blade sinking up to the hilt.

Jaws snapped at him, breathing out a horrendous, humid last gasp right in his face, and then the rat died.

Neil had no time to revel in his victory, because the rats came on in waves. He pulled his sword from the dead rat and slashed at the next one, which squealed in pain and retreated only to return.

But his sword wasn't the only weapon he had. Neil looked at the torch in his hand, and at the greasy, matted fur of the next attacking rat, and swung it at the beast.

It connected with the side, leaving an orange smear on the rat's side. The unfortunate rat hissed and scratched at it, but the flame spread on its side and up its back, but they kept coming anyway.

Neil chopped at the next one, almost severing its head, and then stabbed the one after. They kept coming, wave after wave, and one or two ran past his sword and torch, sinking teeth into his legs before he could kick or stab them away.

Then, it stopped.

Neil blinked, gasping for air. Bodies of rats surrounded him, several still burning, but none of them were still living.

"I did it." His voice sounded odd, echoing around the cave. It was quiet now, no longer filled with the squeal and squeaking of the rats.

He wiped off his sword on the fur of the nearest dead rat, then sheathed it. His body glowed for a moment, the sound of horns triumphant in his ear.

Neil pulled out the amulet quickly, touching its warm metal. The menu swirled into existence, lighting up the cave surrounding him.

Advanced to level 2. Choose your skill.

A thrill ran up his back, a feeling of accomplishment accompanying it. *This is what I need. One more step closer.*

Neil pressed the continue button, the skill screen appearing. Now, at the bottom, the number under "Skill Points" advanced to one.

He had looked at this menu briefly, but hadn't spent much time on it. Now, with the chance to earn something, he was more interested.

It was a tree, starting at a single skill and spreading into a few different paths.

"I guess this makes it easy," he mumbled, the hovered his hand over the level two skill.

"Inner strength." He hovered over it, and another bubble of light materialized into a wall of text. *With the strength of the hero, you gain a fire inside that burns brighter than any star in the sky.*

Somewhere farther into the cave dripped water. *What does that mean?*

He wondered, thinking about having a fire inside. What kind of fire would it be? What would it feel like?

Like anger he felt every time he failed? Or something greater, more pure, something he had wondered about ever since he was a boy?

Neil pressed down, the border around the skill turning silver. A ray of light came out of the amulet, circled him once, then pierced his chest.

Neil cried out in pain, but then realized there was none. The light entered him, and then was gone. Even the menu had disappeared, even though he hadn't dismissed it.

Hands came up to his chest, expecting to find a hole, but instead touching his thick shirt. Beneath his flesh was clean and intact.

I don't feel any different?

But a squeak from down to the left brought him from his thoughts. There were several openings beyond him, the tunnels continued out of the cave.

And, by the sounds of it, so did the rats. Neil shivered, hand instinctively going to his sword.

But he wasn't finished yet. He pulled his knife from his pack and knelt down next to a dead rat.

Farmer Bill had taught him this. He cut into it, skinned the fur from the flesh, collecting all the parts of it he could. There were traders scattered throughout the world who might pay good money for all of it, and it didn't take much time until he had everything useful from the pack of rats tucked into his backpack.

Fur, teeth, meat, and bones. They fit neatly inside, leaving plenty of room for what certainly was more of a fight up ahead.

There were three tunnels leaving the cave, not including the one he had entered from. They were all in complete darkness.

He had to choose one.

10

SHOCK AND JAW

Neil took a moment, looking at each tunnel entrance, then picked the far right.

"Looks like a good place to start." Torch outstretched, Neil knelt down and entered it.

This one was shorter, but it too took him into a cave filled with rats.

They were less surprised by his arrival, and fell upon him all at once. Neil struggled to keep them off, suffering more bite wounds, but managed to kill them all.

There was no leveling this time, but his skill with a blade had gone up. He didn't feel all that much better with his sword, and wondered if he should have picked a different weapon, but put it away and harvested from the rats. This cave had only one entrance.

With only one option left Neil took it. When he was back in the first cave he paused. *Two options left.*

He pulled up his quest progress, wondering if he had finished. While he applied a few bandages to his legs, which started to heal, he glanced at the glowing letters.

Not finished. The other quests he had done turned golden when each task was accomplished. This still was white, with one objective.

Kill all the rats.

Neil took out his last bandage, holding it in his hand. *Should I save it?*

He hadn't anticipated needing this many, or else he would have made more on the island. It would be easy enough to make more when he was off this farm though.

Neil shrugged, then applied it, gaining the last little bit of health he could. He was stronger now than he had been when he entered these caves, and less afraid.

Feeling more confident, he advanced down the left tunnel on a whim. It curved the same direction, and farther down, before ending at another cave.

This time Neil was ready for the onslaught.

Rats rushed at him, but he stayed back in the tunnel, forcing them to come at him one at a time.

Even though he didn't have much room to move, his body nearly taking up the entirety of the tunnel hunched over, he was able to stab well enough, and it was over.

And he hadn't even taken any damage. A smile crept across his face. *Not so hard after all.*

They were bigger too, about double the size of the first two packs of rats.

Something glinted in the light of his torch, catching his eye. Neil stopped harvesting the rats mid stroke, and approached it.

Pushing aside the remains of some smaller creature, and a few gross strands of rat hair, he unearthed a small brass locket.

It was light, and seemed undamaged. He turned it over in the light of the torches, then tucked it into his pack, pleased at the find.

"Might net me a few coins. I'll take it."

After finishing the with rats he went back to the center tunnel, advancing down it with anticipation.

It was longer. Much longer. After a few feet it started to go down at a healthy clip, and shortened too.

Neil could still walk, but his hunch was almost double. He wasn't sure that he could stab a sword well enough, and some of his confidence waned.

It got worse when he got stuck, his broad shoulders caught between two chunks of rock that happened to squeeze the tunnel to a narrow point.

Luckily, a few tugs and he was able to go back. He tried to turn, still standing, but his belly got in the way.

So, Neil got down on his hands and knees and crawled under it, only to be set upon by a rat in hiding on the other side.

It scratched at his eyes, raking sharp points of pain across his face. Neil yelled and lashed out, stabbing forward with his sword.

It bit, sinking into a squealing body, but there were more right behind. He tried to stand, catching another rat with his left hand, who promptly bit into his arm, and tugged his sword free.

The rats came on like waves upon the shore, crashing into him. Neil had nowhere to go, he barely struggled to his knees and was hemmed in behind him by the tunnel.

He hacked and slashed, stabbed at rat and air alike, staring through his eyes burning with sweat that trickled into them.

The smell of blood filled the air, almost making him choke, if it wasn't for the continuous attack.

The stone of the tunnel was hard against his back. It cut into him, but the alternative was to be overwhelmed.

And it didn't seem to let up. No matter how many rats he killed or injured, there always seemed to be another one. His arm grew heavy, his stamina and health dangerously low.

I have to get out of here. I have to escape. The other rooms had at most seven rats, but he had already killed seventeen, and his torchlight flashed in dozens more beady eyes staring back at him in hatred.

His eyes sought an escape pat, anything, that could help him. He swung the torch, catching an advancing rat in the side, and it caught fire and ran away screaming in fear.

If they weren't out to kill him, and the size of a small dog, Neil would have felt worse about it.

As it was, he could barely keep up.

But, by some sheer stroke of luck, the burning rat fled deeper into the cave, giving him enough light to see inside.

And his heart sank even further.

It was a roundish room, all pure rock. A dead end, one that might be the end of him.

He slashed another rat, killing it, and the others stopped coming on. It gave him time to catch his breath just for a moment, then just before the light from the burning rat went out his eyes caught a glimpse of something moving in the corner.

Fear gripped at his heart. This was no oversized rat, this thing was his size or bigger. He squinted into the darkness where he had seen it, hoping it had just been a figment of his imagination.

It was too dark, and the rats surged forward trying to catch him with his defenses down.

Neil wasn't caught unprepared though, lashing shout at the nearest attacker with a downward slash, then bashing another in the snout with his torch.

His back hurt, both from bending over and the sharp rocks behind him. *I have to go forward.*

He wanted to go back, but knew that in the few seconds it would take him to get out on his hands and knees the last little bit of his health would be gone.

He didn't want to die, not in this place, not after coming so far.

So Neil dug deep inside himself, looking for something that he could cling to. Thoughts of Tad's eyes flashed through his mind, and he clutched to it like a man clinging to a log in a raging river.

"Arghh!" Neil screamed and rushed forward, kicking one rat to the left of him, and stabbing at another to his right.

The rats scattered, surprised at the sudden attack and the yell. They retreated into the caved, and Neil was out of the tunnel.

He straightened and raised his torch, shining the flickering firelight into the cave.

He wished he hadn't.

Up rose the shadowy shape, standing taller than he was. the giant rat turned to him, eyes blazing with red rage and bared its long, sharp teeth the size of his hands.

Neil gulped and looked around him. He looked back at the big rat, realizing he had just killed almost all of its litter.

Its eyes flashed, and it let out a scream that was filled with pain and anger.

He didn't need to check his health to know it was low, the red creeping in at the edges of his vision told him he was dangerously close. Every fiber of his being told him to run.

But rats clustered around him, just outside the reach of his sword. They chittered and squeaked, angry beady eyes glaring at him and jaws snapping.

They were waiting for their mother, and they would do anything to keep her safe. He didn't have even a second to look back.

There would be no escape now. Only combat would save him now.

Neil tightened the grip on his sword, praying that he would be able to survive. If he didn't, he would have to start it all over again from his last login point.

There was no wind in the cave. It was hot, humid, and oppressive. It smelled of filth and rotting carcasses and was almost overwhelming to his sense of smell.

The big rat plodded across the cave, its belly and tail dragging on the floor in a scrape like leather on rock. Small rats nipped at her paws, running out of the way.

Neil was her target. Those blazing eyes fixed on him, sharp, pointy teeth bared in anger.

He took a deep breath, and then they were on him.

Three rushed him at once, two more right behind him, going for his ankles. He sliced the one to his right first, stabbing the one on the left while he shoved his torch into the middle one.

It stopped them, but the rats at the back leaped onto their fallen companions and used them to launch at him.

It startled him, forcing him back a step, but he was already at the cavern wall and knocked his head against rock. He gritted his teeth but narrowly managed to get his sword up in time to knock one rat into the other.

Still, they swarmed on. Neil stopped thinking, channeling all he could into his arms and legs. He didn't come out unharmed, the red growing around the edges of his vision as he was scratched and bit.

If only I had some better armor. The thought was fleeting, swept away by another rush of two more rats.

They weren't giving him a way out, and they wouldn't let him round the cave. The mother rat was almost to him now.

There was no escaping it.

Neil was almost overwhelmed by the smaller rats, but the fighting had taken the toll on them too. Less than a half dozen remained.

If I can just get rid of them. And then the mother rat was on him, jaws snapping for his throat.

Sweat running down his forehead, Neil ducked and raked his sword across its flank. She screamed, blood dripping from the cut, but he hadn't cut nearly deep enough to do anything but make her angry.

A tail swept through the air, catching him on the side of his head and knocking him over. Neil grunted, all air leaving his body, and he tried to roll before the smaller ones could reach him.

His torch fluttered, almost going out as it lay in the dirt and refuse laden floor of the cave.

I can't stay here. I have to get up. But his head was swimming from the hit. It didn't feel like a game. It was so real, the pain, the feel of dirt in his mouth, the taste of blood.

The second stretched out into what felt like minutes.

Something bit his calf, and he kicked out, connecting with something. It was what he needed, and he rolled over, scrambling to his feet.

Something brushed across his back. He whirled, shuffling out of the way of another bite from the mother rat.

He decapitated a smaller rat that was too close, then he backed up to give himself room. He was exhausted. All his muscles felt like jelly, and his sword shivered in his shaking hands.

Neil wasn't sure how long he could hold it up. He cursed the fact that what he seemed to be in real life was reflected in this game.

Out of shape. Overweight. Severely lacking in strength.

Another rat came at him, and he thrust at it, but it batted his sword away with a paw. Neil's eyes opened wide as it opened dripping jaws and lunged at him.

He barely brought his sword around in time, falling back on his butt and holding it up.

The rat couldn't stop in time. It fell on his sword, squeaking and screaming in pain, blood dripping down the fuller, then died.

A larger paw raked down his side. The mother rat was back at him.

Neil yelled out and pulled away, rolling back farther into the cave. Pain lanced down his arm a few seconds later.

He grimaced, holding his right arm with his left hand, and fled into the center of the cave. His torch lay on the ground, forgotten in the rush, sputtering and sparking.

The rats didn't seem to mind the dark of the cave and chased him. Three more small ones were still alive, and the mother.

Hand free, Neil steadied his grip on the sword. They were in between him and the exit of the cave, the only way out. He had two hands on the sword now.

It wasn't going to work if he was always on the defensive, and with the small arc of the torchlight fading he only had a few more moments of light left.

In the dark he was toast.

Driven on by Tad's look of desperation Neil let out the biggest roar he could. He leaped forward striking down with a savage blow to the rat in front of him.

It died instantly. The remaining two small rats stopped advancing, and looked hesitant.

Neil seized on his advantage, cutting at one and then the other, dealing life ending cuts to each.

But the mother rat was not afraid, and hissed at him as it turned and swung her tail like a whip at him.

Neil jumped back, catching just the tip across his left side, then rushed back in cutting at the mother rat's flank.

He was rewarded with a line of blood, but it wasn't deep enough to do much damage. Heart pounding, he raised his sword again, but the monster rat turned before he could do anything about it, sinking its jaws into his right wrist.

Neil stood in shock as blood dripped down its jaws. Their eyes met, the torchlight reflecting off the fading black pupils.

It chewed. Pain gripped him then, and he almost dropped the sword, but he pulled back.

The rat came with his hand, still gripped onto his wrist. Claws raked his armored shirt.

Red mist contracted around his vision. *I'm not going to make it.*

He could always come back, redo the whole dungeon again.

No. I have to do this. Anger flared up in him and he caught onto it, fanning it into a flame that drove him.

Instead of retreating, he pressed forward, pushing his arm deeper into its mouth, yelling at the top of his lungs.

It worked.

The rat gagged and let go.

"Die!" Neil let go with his left hand, twisted the blade, and shoved it deep into the rat's open mouth.

The rat tried to pull back, but Neil pressed forward, thrusting as deep as he could.

It tried to scream, but its mouth was filled with blood and sword. The rat thrashed and twitched.

The smell of foul rot and bile mixed with blood flooded out of its mouth. Neil held on, through the red that nearly covered his vision, thrusting forward.

The thrashing slowed, then stopped. The light in the rat's eyes faded.

It was done.

A chime sounded, and the red pulled back in an instant. Neil, still breathing deep with a pounding heart, looked at his wrist that had been mangled seconds earlier.

It was whole, not a scratch or bite mark to speak of. His exhaustion, however, had not gone away and he slumped into a sitting position to rest.

He pulled out his amulet, eager to see what he had advanced in. As the light coalesced he started to smile.

Level 4.

He had skipped an entire level.

Down in the dark, surrounded by the bodies of rats and filth, with his torch on the verge of sputtering out, Neil leaned back and basked in the glow of victory.

11

BACK TO THE CELLAR

When Neil had recovered his breath, and saved his torch from going out, he spent a few minutes going through his new stats to see how he had progressed.

His bladed skill had gone up, as well as his dodge ability, advancing to the next two levels.

"Well on my way." He had expected, since his health had been restored when he leveled up, that his body would recover, but when he moved his muscles protested. He found out it was because his fatigue level had remained high.

I'll have to remember to find a way to recover that. He already knew he could sleep in a bed and it would go down, but it had filled up so quickly since he had woken up this morning. *It must be the combat.*

After gathering supplies from the smaller rats he cut into the mother rat. She had more meat and fur than the others, which took more time to harvest, but it was something else in her stomach that gave him pause.

It was a small thing, a circular band of metal that shined when he rubbed off the bile, but it was not a ring.

He held it up to the torchlight, vaguely recognizing the shape, but he was tired and it didn't come directly to his thoughts so he tucked it away in his money pouch and finished.

When he was done the cave was empty. He searched along the edge, looking for some way the rats had come in, but the only opening he found was the one he had come in. It was the same for the ceiling.

Neil scratched his head, puzzled at where they had come in, then shrugged.

It was probably made this way. Pack heavily loaded, he went back the way he came.

His torch illuminated the farmer's face.

"You made it," he said, with obvious surprise.

Neil furrowed his brow. "I did."

"And they're..."

"I've taken care of them. They won't bother you anymore." The dubious look the farmer gave him annoyed him some, but Neil wanted to get out of the cellar. He climbed the rough ladder up and into the fading glow of evening.

Macgee had a candle lit and burning on the table, apparently interrupted in dinner.

There was only one setting.

"Didn't expect you so soon." The farmer shrugged sheepishly. "Otherwise I would have made you some."

Neil stared at the steaming bowl of stew and decided he didn't need it.

"Let's talk about rewards instead," Neil said, turning to the old man. The scent of the stew lingered in the air, peppery and humid, a stark contrast to the horrible smell of the caves below.

Farmer Macgee cleared his throat. "Right. Well, I'm a poor farmer, and don't have much money to offer, but I've gotten some leeks ready for you as thanks."

"Leeks?" Neil stared at him, dumbfounded.

"Go good in stew, and as flavorful as they come."

"I've never heard of them before." Reality caught up to him. This was a low level quest, the most he was going to get out of it was a few levels.

Still, he expected some money. "I was hoping for..."

"I'll put in a good word for you. You've helped me more than you know." Macgee's eyes dropped to his wringing hands. "Harvest has been bad these last few years and I'm not sure..." He blinked rapidly a few times. "Never you mind about that."

Neil's disappointment faded. He took another look around the small farmhouse, with new seeing eyes.

There were pots scattered around collecting leaks from the roof. All the dishes were dented, scratched, or broken. Although run down, the farmer kept it clean, and the hands of one who cared but just didn't have the means to keep up were evident.

"I'll take the leeks, they probably are the best around."

Farmer Macgee's eyes brightened. "You can be sure of that. They get plenty of water and soak up the sun, making them grow big and fat. I was just about to harvest them when this all happened." He waved around, to his cellar hole.

Neil smiled and listened to him continue to preen about his produce as he followed the old farmer out into the field and the barn beyond.

He kept the leeks inside, and grabbed a big bunchful, thrusting them into Neil's waiting hands.

"Thanks." Neil tested their weight, examined them. They were fat, thicker than most leeks he had seen in real life photos, and every time he touched them they let out a pungent leek smell. "I'm not sure I'll have much room in my pack."

Neil gave them back to the farmer and ruffled through his pack, pulling out a few chunks of rat meat to make room.

"That'll do," Neil said, setting them. "Here, you take this and dispose of it however you want and I'll take those."

Farmer Macgee's eyes widened as soon as he took them. "I can't take this."

"With a little seasoning it wouldn't be that bad."

"No, this would fetch a good price on the market, far more than my leeks." Macgee shook his head. "I wouldn't feel right about it."

"It's the cheapest item I have. I need to keep the hides to sell, and I want the leeks." Neil took them back, stuffing them into his pack and slinging on his shoulder. "Throw them away for all I care, that's what I was going to do with it."

Macgee's eyes softened. He clutched the meat. Neil wondered when the last time he had meat was, but decided against asking about it.

"If ever you need somewhere to stay, my farm is always open to you," Macgee said, taking off his hat and wringing his hands.

Neil looked up into the sky. The sun cast its rays along the bottom edge of the clouds, rippling and shining in a dozen colors of the rainbow. It was just as late his time, and he knew he should be getting to sleep.

It would be a good time to save, and I could recuperate some fatigue. "How about tonight? Do you have room for me?"

Macgee smiled, a single tooth on his bottom left missing. "I'd be obliged."

Epilogue

The transaction complete, the leeks now firmly in his back-pack and the rat meat disappeared somewhere about the farm, Neil settled into his makeshift bed in the hay loft of the barn, he took a chance to sit back and relax, calling up his stats and leafing through them.

He was still woefully weak, and he knew it, but the few levels he had advanced put him in a much better position than he had been just a few short hours ago, and as an early access player he was well above those who would get the game in a few days.

Almost all of his combat stats had advanced something, dodging, health, edged weapons, and even a few of his medical ones were closer to the next advancement than they had been.

It made him feel better, seeing the progress bars fill up, but even that thought brought a twitch of pain. So much different than real life where he couldn't see his progress, if there was any at all.

He shifted in his straw tick, feeling a stray one poke into his back with a sharp lance of pain. It was thick with the smell of hay here, and even a touch of mildew, but it wasn't totally unpleasant.

In fact, he was more comfortable here than in his own bed.

Neil dismissed the menus, leaned back, and stared up at the ceiling.

For what seemed like the first time in his life he felt like he was home.

Eclectic Stories

Thank you for spending your precious time reading this book.

If stories make you salivate, learn more about lore, take an exclusive sneak peek behind the scenes, and get writing updates in my newsletter, Eric's Eclectic Stories.

As a bonus you'll get *Stories from the Deep*, a Patmos Sea Fantasy Adventure anthology that gives a glimpses of lore, extra prologues and epilogues, and character backstories.

If you aren't satisfied, unsubscribe at any time.

Join at erickercher.com.

-Eric Kercher

ALSO BY ERIC KERCHER

Patmos Sea Fantasy Adventure Series

Fathomless Pursuit
Architect's Prize
Ironbound Path
Sunken Prey
Unanswered Prophecy
Hardened Pilgrim
Final Peace

Seventh Hall Chronicles

Seventh Hall
Ode to the Survivors
Bastion of the Deep

Epic of Hornblood Castle

Siege of the Unfinished Keep
Winter at Hornblood
Branch of the Everlong

Castlebound Adventures

Rats in the Cellar!

Anthologies

Red Eagle Anthology
Searchlight Anthology

About Author

Eric Kercher was born and raised in a small town on the Great Plains on good books. After attending a small state school on the east coast he joined the US Navy to serve his country and explore the world. He worked on submarines, and the world beneath the waves captivated him with all its mysteries and wonders. After spending time in larger cities, he's settled down in a quiet town with his wife and children. When not on an adventure in a good book the author enjoys creating dust woodworking, architecture, and spending time with loved ones.

Find out more at www.erickercher.com.